THE PATH OF PRIDE

A PREQUEL TO THE DESTROYER'S WRATH

N. P. COOPER

NATIONAL
LIBRARY
OF AUSTRALIA

A catalogue record for this work is available from the National Library of Australia

FOR ALL THOSE WHO ENCOURAGED ME ALONG
THE WAY.

JERA

BULWARK ISLANDS

GREAT NORTH OCEAN

NORTHWATCH

HARVERNESS

ASMERE

NESTARN

ICE RA

KARVER

STONEKEEP

MIRALTHRALL

CORDOVA

CLEARBROOK

DANAREL

MIRALLYN RIVER

HILLCREST

RAILAIN

HEARTLAND'S GATE

SEALCOVE

LAKE PRISTINE

GREENTREE LAKE

ROLLING HILLS

DARK IRON MOUNTAINS

THE BONE COAST

LAKETOWN

CLIFFSIDE

MIDLAN

WESTERN PORT

GUILTOWN

WESTERN WATERS

SOUTHP

THREE SEAS

TO AVSAN

SEA

TO JERANAH

N

NGARA

HENMAR'S POINT

MOUNT WHISPERWIND

TERRALIV HOMELAND

CLAIREMONT

GES

PERESET

CONCLAVE CITY

THE JADE COAST

GRANDEIL

JEPHSTAT

MIDWAY

DAMERETTE

ON RIVER

THE WRAITH WOODS

CARUEL

RIVER'S BEND

FOX HEAD LAKE

ARAMAR

CAMAR RIVER

TO SUNSET ISLES

SEA

THE EMERALD SEA

ARBORII HOMELAND

EASTERN WATCH

SILVERTOWN

OAKVIEW

SEA OF DREAMS

AN'S LANDING

AIDEN'S INLET

FISHES

MARASDAN

"No matter how insane, no matter how hopeless, no matter how many we lose on the journey, we must continue to move forward. Nothing remains behind us but dust…"
Excerpt from the log of Admiral Chain, Commander of the Desolate Fleet.

CHAPTER I

AFTERMATH

She woke to the sight of a clear blue sky, and a flock of vultures wheeling overhead.

The pain came next.

Every part of her body felt as though an Imbic mutation had pummelled it. She turned her head and rolled stiffly onto her right side. How long had she lain here, unconscious and helpless? Long enough for the vultures to find her, that much was certain.

To find them, she corrected. Beside her lay the body of a man in perhaps his forties, eyes glassy and still. There was no life there. However she had ended up here, she hadn't been the only one.

She struggled to her knees, the movement startling some of the giant carrion feeders which perched nearby. They scattered enough for her to see another body, dressed all in black with a good silver-lined cloak, torn and pierced where the vultures had begun their feast.

What is happening here?

She looked to her other side, only to be confronted by

the startling sight of four more corpses within the immediate area. Again, all were dressed in black, with varying colours adorning the lining of their well-made cloaks. Two had silver, one blue, another white. She felt that should mean something, but her mind refused to make the connection.

Her heart began racing as she realised she did not know how she had arrived here, or worse, who these people were. She stopped moving for a long moment. They weren't the only ones she couldn't recognise.

Who am I?

She looked at herself for a long moment, comparing herself to the others. She was dressed as they were. Black clothes over which a good cloak with a deep blue lining sat bunched around her shoulders. Her hands were soft, not those of a manual labourer, and her shoes were new, or close to it. Not a traveller then. She forced herself to examine the bodies of the others. Their garb and general features agreed with her own.

Whoever these people are, I'm one of them. Why can't I remember them? Why Can't I remember myself?

She searched her mind for a name and found an expanse of emptiness large enough to swallow the world.

Pushing that uncomfortable image down deep, she struggled to her feet. The stiffness was starting to wear off now, and with it went some of the pain. With that increased awareness came also the realisation of just how far she was from any sort of help. The surrounding area was wild in the truest sense.

Sharp jutting rocks stuck out from the grassy ground at irregular intervals, and large trees whose first branches sat thirty spans above the ground dominated the area.

Behind one of the rocks, another pair of feet was visible.

How many of us ended up here? And why am I the only one alive?

As she watched the feet, one of them jerked. It seemed an involuntary movement, but the thought that she might not be alone out here drove her closer. As she rounded the concealing rock, a shiver of dread worked its way up her spine as a beige tail, topped with a tuft of darker fur lashed languidly into view.

Lion. How do I know that name, but not my own?

She backed away slowly. Survivor or not, she had no means of dealing with such a beast.

A stick snapped beneath her feet, and the tail stopped.

In the blink of an eye, a colossal body sprung up to crouch on the obscuring rock. The sheer magnitude of it was terrifying, even without the red smear of blood around its mouth. The lion's head was triple the size of her own even without the mane, and its body was a study in graceful, muscled perfection. For a long heartbeat it sat there, unblinking as it considered the new arrival, its intense stare doing nothing to ease her mind.

She backed away a few steps as the lion watched. She wanted to scan the ground, the bodies, anywhere for a weapon she could defend herself with, but only their continued locked gaze seemed to be keeping the huge predator at bay. She didn't even want to blink.

A sound off to the left caught the lion's attention.

She took the chance to put a few more steps between them.

Whatever attracted the lion's attention didn't hold it for long. On her third step, it swivelled its giant head back toward her. It regarded her for an instant before opening its bloodied jaws to let out an ear-shattering roar, one that sent her fleeing in the opposite direction.

She hadn't made it ten spans when she heard the thundering footsteps behind her. She looked frantically to the left and the right for any means of escape, but there was nothing other than the sharp head-high rock formations and straight trunked trees. The area was equally void of anything she could use as a weapon. There was a large branch thirty spans to her left, but she would never make it that far.

She took an instant to glance over her shoulder as she ran, and was horrified to see the lion had already closed the distance. It began a powerful leap that would end their short chase.

In a primitive reflex, she brought her hands up to fend off the giant beast, and at the moment it made contact, a wall of shimmering, translucent blue appeared between them. The lion howled in pain even as it knocked her flat, sliding across the shimmering wall of light to tumble to the ground several spans away. The huge cat roared again, though this time in pain. It turned and limped away, favouring its front right paw and leaving a thin trail of blood in its wake.

What was that?!

Even as her focus shifted from the lion to the shimmering blue light, it vanished as abruptly as it arrived. Thankfully, the lion kept walking.

As she sat up, nursing a new bruise on the back of her head, she noticed a strange object on the grass next to her. She picked it up and turned it over, only then realising that it was a pair of claws. A pair of claws with half the toes still attached. She glanced back at the lion as it limped down the decline, disappearing from view beyond a rock pile.

Somehow she had done… something to it. She looked at her hands, and at her clothes, but nothing seemed out of the ordinary. There was little to be found in her pockets, other than a paper wrapped candy with a picture of a strawberry on it. Nothing at all to explain that shimmering blue light. From beyond her sight line, the lion roared again. It seemed their brief tussle had been enough for it for now, given the result, and the feline appeared to be moving off in earnest. She sat there for a minute longer, catching her breath as her heart returned to a somewhat normal speed, and examining the severed toes. They looked untouched apart from the actual injury, which was as straight and precise as any cut she could imagine. But what had caused it? She looked around again, but there was no one else nearby. Whatever had happened, she had done it herself. But how?

Apart from sheer curiosity, there were clearly dangerous animals around here, wherever here was, and exactly how she had fended it off would be an excellent thing to know.

Hesitating for a moment, she took the two claws with her. They would be a poor weapon in her hands, but right now they were all she had.

Scanning the area, it appeared she was now alone apart from the few vultures which hadn't scattered when the lion pounced. And the bodies. She stopped for a moment, considering. She didn't know these people, or she hoped she didn't. It didn't feel right to just leave them here. Unfortunately, she lacked the means either to dig graves or cut wood for a pyre. That didn't leave many options, and despite the frequently occurring stone formations, there were nowhere near enough loose rocks to build a cairn for all of them.

She sighed as she approached the first body. There were few injuries visible other than a broken arm and a depression that might indicate a fractured skull. It was strange. There were no tears in his clothes or grass stains to suggest the man had been in a fight, but clearly something had bested him.

After a moment of indecision, she checked his pockets. She still didn't know where she was, or how long it would take to return to more civilised lands. Anything she could find would be useful at this point. She came up empty, which was a little strange in itself.

Moving from one body to the next, she found similar injuries on all the others. The bodies which the lion and vultures had been feasting on she discounted. There was no way to tell which wounds were caused by them, and which had been common to whatever had brought them all here. The strange thing was that most of the injuries she could identify were on the back. Not the back of the bodies, though, as though they had been running away, or ambushed. These were all broken bones, which she had to turn the bodies over to find. All facing the ground. It was almost as though someone had dropped them from a great height. She looked back at where she had woken. There was an abnormal amount of leaves around the patch. She looked up. The tree shadowing the position had several large broken branches swinging from it about twenty spans up. She hissed out a breath. No wonder her ribs were so sore. It was the Maker's own luck that she hadn't broken every bone in her body falling from up there. With nothing to slow the others' falls, it was no marvel only she had survived. How they had come to be in that situation was something her mind wasn't ready to process just yet.

Numbly moving to the last few bodies, she checked their pockets and came up with a sandwich wrapped in a thin oiled cloth with floral patterning. The old man she took it from had a severe cast to his features and she doubted the cloth was his. The items were odd, just snacks. It was almost as if they had been out for a carefree morning stroll, not bothering to take anything else with them as they expected to be home before lunch.

Then this.

She tucked the oiled cloth with its sandwich into one of her pockets before noticing the plain silver ring on his left hand. There was nothing remarkable about it as far as jewellery went, only the finger he wore it on made it important. She nodded to herself. This man had been married, the floral cloth with its sandwich likely something his wife had made him before he left the house.

If that were true, if they'd met up somewhere, she'd probably known him, known his wife even. She took the ring.

Moving around the area, she began the arduous task of laying them next to each other. She could do little else. But with the realisation that some or all of these people may have been her friends, she felt the need to do that much, at least. As she finished arranging the bodies, she examined them more closely for personal trinkets which their families might want returned. There were three more wedding rings and two necklaces of varying quality, along with a tiny wooden horse statue she had missed before. One that appeared as though it belonged to a child.

When she was finished with the distasteful task, she stood.

It was well past midday according to the sun, and despite her confusion and pain, she couldn't remain here overnight. There was no shelter to be found, no water, and only the food she had discovered in their pockets.

It was time to move on.

"Sometimes secrets remain well hidden. Sometimes they do not, and shake the very foundations of our lives. The bigger the secret, the more lives are shaken. Mine shook a world."
Excerpt from the trial of Eldrik the Black.

CHAPTER 2

CONSEQUENCE

The sparse vegetation and low rock formations did nothing to hide the terrain, which sloped gradually upward to the east. It wasn't enough to chart a course. To find her way home, she would have to first determine where in Jeranon she was, then she could decide on which direction to travel. Wherever she was, the trees were unfamiliar, and that didn't bode well.

There was only one decision to make, and she began walking uphill, heading for a mountainous outcropping of rock at the summit of the hill. It was going to take hours, and she didn't know what she would find when she got there.

As she continued walking, her already pummelled legs protesting, she kept a wary eye out in case the lion decided to come back for more. Or in case some other lurking beast noticed her passage. The afternoon was cool in a way she was not used to, and now and then the slight tang of salt crept into her nostrils.

I must be near the sea.

But which direction was it? To all rights, the sea should

be north, but this coastline was utterly unfamiliar, and the slope of the land headed down towards the west. Hopefully, the peak would grant her some much-needed clarity. If the sea really was to the west... well, she wasn't going to think about that right now. An hour later, she reached the top of the hill and stood below the sheer rock outcropping. There was no chance she could climb it in her already battered condition. To the north, the way looked easier, so she headed around the hill until she rounded the outcropping. It was still a hundred spans straight up, but time and wind and a long-ago earthquake had conspired to present a far rougher surface than that on the east wall. There was a clear path to the top, and although the ancient landslide led deeper into a crevasse, the sky was visible at the top. With a short sigh, she pulled herself up over the first broken boulder. A small lizard darted away from her hand, and she jumped. The little creature had been so well camouflaged she had almost crushed it without realising. She scaled the next boulder and the next before having to work her way around the base of a tree which had wedged its way into a crack and begun growing there decades, or maybe even centuries, before. It was hard going. The walls of the crevasse were covered in clumps of moss and lichen that made for treacherous footing, but it seemed she was quite fit, and her footing remained firm.

Another hour passed as she climbed hand over foot up the broken facing of the cliff. She startled again when a bird shot from a nest nestled into a crack and called out a raucous song that echoed in the confined space. She couldn't help but laugh at the fright. If it weren't for being injured and alone, the climb might even have been fun. Almost at her destination, she looked around for another handhold. She was less than ten spans from the summit, and she had run out of rocks.

Blast.

From its base, the pile of rocks looked like they had reached the summit, but there was still some work to do. The sides of the crevasse were a lost cause, smooth and covered with moss. Where they met, however, might offer an opportunity. Wedging herself into the gap, she placed her hands in front and behind her and pushed up, quickly jamming her feet in as well. The crevasse was little more than a foot wide, but between her hands, back, and feet, she was able to gain enough leverage to force her way upwards an inch at a time. Exhausted, she took hold of the lip of the cliff and pulled herself the rest of the way up. Rolling away from the edge, she took a moment to lay flat on her back in the afternoon sunshine while she recovered her breath.

With any luck she would be high enough to see the ocean. She was sure she had smelled it earlier. That should at least tell her something.

Just don't be to the west, her mind added fearfully.

She looked up at the sun, taking her bearings, and sat up.

To the west was a great expanse of ocean, broken with a single jutting island, one which might just be within reach. For a long moment, she sat there, stunned.

I'm dead.

There was only one place where an ocean lay to the west, and if she were there, it was a thousand leagues through enemy territory to return home. It was entirely possible she was seeing lands which no human eye had ever beheld. This far west, she wouldn't even have to worry about the Augrahl Imperium or the Northern Plainsmen. The Imbic might be a threat, but legend had it that even they stayed away from this deserted region of the continent. They didn't want to intrude into oo'vi dominion any more than she did. The Blood Forest was purported to have trees which stood a mile high and moved as the sun went down. The entire nomadic species shifting from one location to the next as the oo'vi nestled like parasites within. She felt a shiver run up her back. Perhaps she would be safe out here on the islands? It was unlikely the vast trees could cross a salt ocean. Perhaps wherever she had ended up was remote enough that even Jeranon's most distant enemies might not find her.

She didn't know if that thought was comforting or not.

Her shoulders sank as she realised there were only two options available to her. Either she could try to return home, most likely being killed by the western nations in the process, or she could remain here in exile. The idea of spending the rest of her life alone and in hiding was not a pleasant one, and right now, she needed more information.

To the north, there was nothing. An ocean as wide as the world encompassed the horizon. Her shoulders sank. It was time to see how far from the mainland she was. She turned to the east and felt her jaw drop as she took in the sight.

Before her lay several more islands of varying sizes and elevations, all covered in copious amounts of vegetation other than one cliff face, which stood black and charred with volcanic rock. Beyond them was ocean. Just ocean. Where was the mainland? Where was the mighty continent shared by Jeranon and all the western nations?

Where am I? she once again thought, this time with a great deal more trepidation.

Looking south, there were fewer islands, and those that existed were smaller and further apart. There was a smudge on the horizon, but she couldn't tell from this distance whether it was land or a weather system moving in. Whatever it was, it extended to the limits of her sight.

If the discolouration on the horizon was in fact land to the south, that meant she was on an island chain to the north of the mainland. She clung desperately to that possibility as a name bloomed in her mind.

The Bulwark Islands! I'm on the Bulwark Islands!

I'm not dead...

For several long moments all she could do was sit there and raggedly breathe. She could hear the blood pounding in her temples at the realisation that she was not beyond hope. The Bulwark Islands were distant, and she would need a ship to return to the mainland, but neither were they deserted. There was a garrison located on the shores of the westernmost island where it could oversee the ocean for dozens of leagues. From memory, the garrison wasn't large, and existed purely to warn Jeranon if the western nations attempted a naval incursion. But it would have a ship.

She stood to get a better view. Somehow, she would need to make her way to that large island to the west. She didn't think she could swim there in her current condition. If she could find some food and fresh water though, and stay away from predators, a day or two of rest might correct that situation. She was a strong swimmer. For some reason she remembered that. As she walked to the edge of the outcropping, she finally got a better view of the shoreline. There was perhaps a mile of ocean from beach to beach between the western island and her current landmass. A lot would depend on the current. It would be better to make a raft than swim the distance, but with no tools available, that wasn't going to happen. She would just have to chance the swim.

It started as a feeling.

She looked at the ground, a slight vibration was registering through her feet. She had a momentary flash of panic as her mind recalled the lava encrusted cliff behind her. She looked around as a base rumbling began echoing all across the island. Trees began shaking abruptly, and she was hurled off her feet as the ground lurched below her.

Scrambling away from the cliff edge, she crawled as best she could as the world continued shaking. She couldn't help an involuntary shout of fear as another violent lurch knocked her flat. The far edge of the crevasse crumbled away before her eyes, and a large tree fell from the edge with a snap barely heard over the grinding of the ground. All she could do was lay flat and hang on to the surrounding grass, hoping against hope the rest of the plateau didn't follow it into the ocean.

The shaking went on for almost a minute before it finally subsided, leaving cracks like spiderwebs across the plateau.

What was that?!

Obviously, it had been an earthquake, but she had never felt a tremor even remotely close to the ferocity of the one she had just experienced. She dragged herself to her feet, though whether it was the ground or her still shaking from terror, she could no longer tell.

There was not a tree still standing on the plateau, and the western island seemed to have fared little better. A quarter of its vegetation lay askew, and the entire western face of its main rise had slumped into the ocean. She walked a few hesitant steps closer to the edge, attempting to assess the damage to her own island, and was horrified by what lay below.

What is happening to the ocean?

For the entire length of the gap between the two islands, the ocean had withdrawn, or the land below had risen. And it wasn't just there. All across the island chain, the water which separated them was retreating, revealing the rocky seabed below. She watched on in horror as the retreating sea suddenly stopped as though changing its mind. The ocean abruptly reversed its momentum and sped back towards the islands in a massive wave that would dwarf the tallest trees once it came ashore. The southernmost island was a small one, a low-set rock beach with a large copse of trees at its centre. The wave simply washed over it, flattening every living thing and submersing the entire landmass without slowing. Her heart began hammering again. She looked around wildly for somewhere safer to be, but she was already at the highest point of the island. One of the highest in the entire chain, by the looks of it. There was nowhere else to go. She watched in awe as the wave reclaimed the exposed seabed without mercy. That land had been the ocean's, and it wanted it back. The wave reached the next island with a similar result, and then the next. This island was a little higher though, and as the wave passed over it, the jutting top remained exposed, though cleansed of all terrestrial life.

She could hear it now. A distant thunder that grew as the wave approached. It slammed into another island, and although this one was far bigger, the wave crested it nonetheless. The water shoved and pushed its way around the far side of the island, immersing the low-lying areas until only the upper northern region was still above water.

It was coming for her next.

Her island was far higher than any of the previous ones. Thank the Maker that she'd chosen to climb for a better view of the area instead of heading down towards the beach. Surely she would be safe up here?

The wave slammed into the coastline far below, not even slowing as it tore trees and rocks from their moorings and flooded the entire landmass in an instant. The wave continued coming, up and up it rose, forced on by the pressure of water behind it as it surged up the slope. With a force that shook the plateau, the wave slammed into the rock outcropping a hundred spans below. Even up here, a cold spray whistled up the cliff and soaked her cloak, sending her scrambling for cover. For long minutes she could feel the vibration of the water shoving itself against her clifftop refuge. She moved away from the edge once again, and crouched near the centre, desperately hoping the cracked surface didn't give way.

Eventually, the vibration subsided, and only the spray from the initial crash of the wave had reached the summit. She was alive.

She got to her feet hesitantly, still half expecting the ground to buck at any moment, but whatever natural fury had caused the overwhelming destruction seemed to have been sated. At least for now. Inching her way towards the edge, it was hard to believe what she was seeing. The wave was gone now, having reached the far edge of the islands and travelling further out to sea. Nothing of it remained except the unimaginable destruction left in its wake.

The southern island was simply gone, washed away to the point that whatever was left of it was not enough to remain above the waves.

The next two islands remained, but were scoured of life, and appeared to no longer be anything more than bedrock. To the south, the third island had taken the full brunt of the wave. If its low-lying areas were any indication, all that remained of its vegetation was on the sheltered northern slopes where a section of trees and grass had held tight.

The western island was in somewhat better condition. It sported a set of sheer cliffs on its southern face, which appeared to have somewhat blunted the wave's fury. There was still plenty of damage, but it wasn't scoured clean like the others. Of the slumped rock and dirt the earthquake had thrown into the sea, there was no sign.

Not trusting the integrity of the plateau any more than she had to, she crawled the last few spans to the edge and peered over the cliff to see how her own island had fared.

It wasn't good.

As with the other islands, the beach and low-lying areas had been scoured to bedrock, but the island's elevation had protected a good part of the vegetation further up the slopes. If the other islands were anything to go by, the northern face would be in slightly better shape. The one bit of good news was that there were any number of trees, branches, and other random material now washing up on the beaches.

Some of it must be good for making a raft.

Just the thought of going down there now terrified her. What had caused the earth to shake like that? This part of Jeranon wasn't prone to earthquakes. Her memory was sketchy at best, but she didn't think disasters of this magnitude happened at all. Not here at any rate. What if it happened again?

She looked up at the sky. The sun was where it should be. Her mind insisted that it should have been hours, but in reality only minutes must have passed since the first tremor began. It didn't seem real. One thing was sure, she wasn't about to pick her way down a slippery, wet crevasse deep in the afternoon's shadow. She looked around. There were enough broken branches from the felled trees to make a crude shelter if she used one of the trunks as a windbreak. It would have to do. Backing away from the edge, she got to her feet and began dragging branches and leaves over to the spot she had chosen. There was no way to build a fire, and no fresh water, but at least she still had the oilskin-wrapped sandwich to keep her company.

By the time she finished building the makeshift shelter, the sun was setting, and she was wet, cold, and exhausted. She took out the dead man's sandwich and said a silent thanks to whoever had packed it for him. Eating half of it, she savoured the thinly sliced roast beef and cheese. She wanted to devour it all, but there was no telling when she would have access to more food. She re-wrapped the second half after a moment's hesitation and placed it back in a pocket, then lay down and promptly fell into an exhausted sleep.

Flesh is irrelevant, only the soul holds meaning.
Imbic Proverb.

CHAPTER 3

THE DISTANT LIGHT

The sky was once again bright, and large buildings stood all around. A dog barked somewhere in the distance and a young vendor pulling a handcart called out that his pies were hot and delicious. Two for a crown.

She felt in her pockets, but today's excursion would be a short one and she had neglected to bring even a single coin. Her shoulders slumped slightly, and the vendor continued on his way.

Why was she so hungry? She'd only just left home,

The bustle of the city surrounded her. The day was hot, and she was wearing a cloak.

This is what I woke up in, she thought as she remembered the strange dream. There had been a lion, and a tsunami, and several of her colleagues dead in a field.

She shuddered. What madness had made her conjure up that imagery?

Today was important, vital even. Her presentation would justify years of intense research, but she hadn't thought herself so rattled as that.

A vendor walked past, pulling his cart and offering pies for all who could pay.

She frowned, hadn't that boy just gone the other way?

No one took him up on his offer and he continued on. The smell was outstanding, and her stomach rumbled.

She felt around in the pockets of her black tunic and her hand hit something almost at once. It was a silver crown.

Where did that come from? She was sure it hadn't been there a moment ago.

She took off in the direction the boy had taken his cart. He couldn't have gone too far.

She rounded the corner into an open area, paved with sandstone blocks and surrounded on all eight sides by a metal lattice framework. Of the boy and his pies, there was no sign. In fact, the entire courtyard was empty. Empty and silent. She spun. Why had the city gone quiet? She looked around the bustling street she had been on only a moment before, but instead of the press of bodies and aromas of the markets, there was nothing. The stalls were gone, the people vanished.

"That's impossible," she heard herself say, but the evidence was right there in front of her eyes. The street might as well have been made yesterday, even the grime was missing.

The sound of an argument floated to her ears. Again she spun, heading back to the octagonal courtyard.

"I'm telling you it will work, Joram," a middle-aged woman with auburn hair said to her companion.

The older man nodded his balding head and turned at her approach. She stopped in her tracks. It was the same man she had taken the sandwich from in her dream. He was wearing the same clothes as the woman, black tunic and trousers, with a silver-lined cloak. But who was this Joram?

He smiled when he saw her. An open, honest smile.

"So, today is the big day. Are you ready to put us on the map, Johanna?"

She woke, chilled to the bone beside a large fallen tree trunk. The smell of ocean salt registered, and then the words the old man had spoken.

Johanna! My name is Johanna.

She frantically searched her memory for more, but the dream was fading fast.

"Johanna," she repeated over and over again. "Johanna."

The word was all she knew about herself, and she was not about to lose it.

She sat up, her limbs stiff from the cold despite the makeshift pile of foliage she had tried to use as a blanket. The waning moon was high in a cloudless sky, and this far from civilisation, every star in the heavens was glowing. The great mass of the galaxy spread above her, a stark field of illumination cutting through the sky. As she sat there, her legs began to tingle, and Johanna realised she needed to move. The cold and damp from the wave had numbed her extremities to dangerous levels. She stood with difficulty, using the tree trunk to support her weight while her legs circulated enough blood to get her moving. She could feel her toes again now. That would be a good thing once the pins and needles went away.

It took a minute, but once the discomfort receded, she began pacing the plateau. The tsunami and earthquake's violence had felled every last tree up here. Down below, it would be much worse.

She wondered if the lion had survived. If it had, it would be afraid, and on edge. Not exactly a stowaway she wanted to be stuck with.

In the morning, she would have to leave the relative safety of this plateau and search for some way across to the large island. If there was anyone still alive to help her, they would be there, at the garrison.

She walked towards the eastern edge of the grassy outcrop. The wind was stronger out here. She would dry, but could she afford the chilling that would entail? Already her face felt flushed from the cold air, and the moon told her this night was little more than half over. The coldest hours would be yet to come.

She was too excited to sleep again, though. She had a name, and so did the balding man whose wedding band she could now return to his wife. Joram. If the dream were to be believed, they had known each other. He had mentioned research, and given the similarities in their clothing, it was likely they had been part of the same organisation. There were subtle differences though. His cloak had sported a silver lining, hers had blue. Was that relevant, or a personal choice? The dream had offered no such clues.

As she mused, her wandering took her closer to the edge of the plateau facing the large island to the west. She stopped in her tracks, all thoughts of the dream erased as a small fire was revealed a third of the way up the island's slope. It didn't appear natural, and hadn't spread.

Someone's there!

"Help!" Johanna shouted instinctively before realising the distance was far too great for her voice to travel.

She had to get across to that other island before whoever made that fire left.

She ran back to the crevasse she had climbed this afternoon, but the mossy rocks were black in the night, slippery and unforgiving. Trying them now would likely end with a broken bone within a dozen steps, or worse.

Growling in the back of her throat, Johanna knew she would never safely make it back to ground level in the dark. She looked around, but the plateau offered no other possibilities for descent unless she learned how to fly. It didn't seem likely she could achieve that before dawn, so with a scowl she returned to her fallen log-and-branch nest to hide from the biting wind. The moment the first hint of dawn breached the eastern sky, she intended to be on her way. She would climb down this mountain and find whoever remained alive on the western island. Certainly the soldiers at the garrison would help her return to civilisation. There was just the small matter of a mile of open ocean in between them.

"The ocean possesses many a danger. Foremost of these is the water itself."
Excerpt from the log of Admiral Chain, Commander of the Desolate Fleet.

CHAPTER 4

THE GREAT JOURNEY

Day had broken. It was time.

Johanna stretched as she stood. The cold and damp of the night had stiffened her already aching muscles, and several knots had formed in her back, shoulders, and calves. It didn't matter. Today she had an ocean to cross.

She fished in her pockets for the hard candy she had taken from one of her dead colleagues. The small, oiled paper carried the imprint of a red-ripe strawberry. Pulling gently from both ends, the twist of paper unravelled, revealing a light pink confection as hard as a rock. She popped it in her mouth, savouring the flavour as she contemplated the task before her. The crevasse had survived without damage at this end. The sight was a relief. If the pile of debris had collapsed, she had no idea how else she might have climbed down from here.

As it was, the task was not trivial. After lowering herself until she was only gripping the plateau with her hands, she found it impossible to climb down using the same method she had adopted on the way up. There simply wasn't a way to gain the same leverage in this direction.

She looked down. Below her, the first boulder was large and flat, and a full three spans below her feet. It was a long drop, longer than she was tall. There was little choice though. She could either make a controlled jump, or try the climb, risking an awkward fall and injury if she slipped. Both options were risky. If she broke a leg or twisted an ankle, it was over. She would never make the rest of the climb to the ground, let alone reach the other island.

With her hands tiring, Johanna pushed off from the wall and let go. She bent her knees, and quicker than she expected, hit the boulder below, collapsing awkwardly onto her side.

I'm okay.

She picked herself up, surveying the next drop. It was nowhere near as substantial, and she clambered from one rock formation to the next, and then the next. It was midmorning by the time she reached solid ground. There had been a few loose rocks, and the surfaces at the lower level had become slick with retained moisture. But she made it down alive, and without any broken bones to show for it. She would take that for a win.

She looked around nervously as her feet touched the ground. All around her were signs of destruction. Rocks had shifted from where they'd lain for millennia, trees were shattered and laying on their sides, and soil had been churned to muck, or scoured from the bedrock entirely. The one good thing she saw was that the lion was nowhere in sight.

Hopefully the wave carried it away.

She felt bad thinking it, but she still had no means of fighting the creature off if they encountered one another again.

The ground gradually sloped down towards the sea in the west, and for that she was grateful. The swim to the western island would have been much longer otherwise. Keeping a close eye out, she began walking.

It was a short walk, no more than an hour, before she caught sight of the beach, or what remained of it. Instead of sand, innumerable trees were washed up along the stripped shore, a massive tangle of trunks, branches, and foliage from both this and other islands. The trunks stood at crazy angles, both in and out of the current water line. Some even had their roots facing the sky as if some vast child had randomly pushed them into the landscape as decorations for a mile long sandcastle.

It only took a moment to see that many of the smaller logs were floating. Johanna sighed again in relief. She was a strong swimmer, but a mile of open ocean would test anyone. Also, there was no telling what kind of carnivorous marine life existed in this area. She made her way down to the shore. A few birds circled overhead, but other than that, there was only the pulsing of the waves to break the silence. She looked out at the other island. From above, the distance hadn't seemed too great, from down here though the perspective had changed. The water was smooth and clear, but the mile she had estimated was conservative at best.

Halfway up what used to be a pristine beach, a vast tangle of flotsam rested near the shoreline. Johanna headed for it. She would need materials to make a raft, and it seemed a likely spot to find what she needed without traipsing all over the island. As she walked along the shore, something caught her eye. All across the embankment lay hundreds of dead fish, no doubt washed up here and stranded by the tsunami surge as it passed. She stopped for a minute to pick one up from a deeply shady spot. She wasn't familiar with the species, but it was about a foot long with silvery scales on top and a whitish flesh on its belly. Taking a moment to strip a piece of vine from a nearby trunk, she tied the fish to one end. Continuing towards the debris tangle, she added three others. They wouldn't last long before spoiling, but at least she would have food for today if she could manage a fire.

She arrived at the tangle soon after, and dug away a patch of dirt with a nearby stick. Burying the fish in the cool dirt, she covered them over and set about her task. Looking at the sky, she gave herself three hours to build the raft if she wanted to attempt crossing the water before nightfall. If it took longer than that, she would have to launch in the morning. Being caught on the ocean at night on what was sure to be a poorly made raft was not an experience she was looking for.

It didn't take long for her to free a few dozen logs and drag them into the water. Most were made of a wood that floated well, and were light to carry. A few sank straight away, but she soon learned the difference in the wood types, and left those alone. What she needed was rope, or something that would work as such for a few hours. She wasn't building a ship. If the raft survived to the halfway point, she was confident she could swim the rest if need be.

Searching through the debris, she discovered a length of vine of the same variety she had used on the fish. She tugged on it as hard as she could, and the strand came away from the pile without breaking, moving several of the light logs in the process.

This will do.

She began arranging the logs as best she could. Ten went into the body of the raft, just long enough for her to sit or stand on. Two longer ones flanked them, protruding from front and back to help with stability, while another two fulfilled the same function to the sides. At each of the four extremities she added a short log to keep the spacing and help with buoyancy, and began tying them with the vine. She had barely started when she ran out, and there was no more in the pile. Already over an hour had passed, and Johanna sighed. She would need to search the area for more. Much more.

Now that she knew what she needed, it didn't take long to discover a fallen tree hidden over a rocky rise, which until yesterday would have been covered by sand dunes. The trunk was covered in the stuff, and while being quite strong, the fibrous lengths came away from the dead trunk with a decent pull. When she had gathered as much as she could carry, she turned and headed back to the raft. What she found caused her to freeze.

Sniffing at her work was a three-toed lion.

The massive cat lifted its head, turning towards her. Johanna stood stock still as it looked her in the eye. She contemplated running, but where could she go? She might make it to the water and start swimming. It was all she had. The lion took a step towards her, limping badly. She frowned, whatever she had done to its toes during their first encounter hadn't injured it to that extent. The lion let out a roar, but it was a half effort. One which cut off abruptly as the grand cat collapsed onto its chest, panting rapidly as though out of breath.

Johanna frowned. Her heart racing, but not to the extent it had been a moment ago. She dropped the pile of vines and looked the animal over. Circling cautiously towards the water at a safe distance, she finally got a look at its other side. There was a large gash running along most of the length of its flank.

She suspected it wasn't a wound the cat could recover from, and as it lethargically watched her progress without rising, she was starting to wonder if it would die right there.

For long moments she waited at the shore. She didn't want to swim from here if she could help it, but the lion had collapsed just spans away from her raft. It seemed a stupid risk to go back to it. She glanced at the sky, either way, time was running out and this was a complication she didn't need.

She bent down, never taking her eyes off the big cat, and felt the water. Her shoulders slumped. It was freezing. She had thought she could swim across, but with water that cold it wasn't just a lack of energy that might see her fail. The temperature itself would hamper her as it chilled her muscles, slowing her movements and causing her arms and legs to cramp. She would have to make the raft work.

She looked at the construction again, and at the cat which seemed to have lost interest in her now as it licked what it could reach of the wound. Every now and then a shudder would run across the creature. She had a feeling the gash wasn't its only injury.

Backing away from the shore, she headed back to her pile of vines whilst watching for any sign of movement from the lion. It stiffened abruptly, three of its legs splaying out as it scrabbled for a moment in the dirt before becoming still. Its eyes were closed, and it was still breathing, but it was also clearly no longer the threat it had been. Whatever damage the tsunami had done to it must be more extensive than she could tell by looking at its exterior.

Johanna picked up the vine pile and headed around the back of the debris to where she could approach the raft without walking past the unconscious predator. She knelt down quietly and began freeing vines to tie the raft together. Thankfully the big cat didn't seem to have interfered with her work other than to sniff it in investigation.

Johanna tested every thin vine before adding them to the raft, moving with efficiency as she attempted to complete the work before the lion woke. Her hands were not steady as she tied the knots. Any other time she might have cursed in frustration.

Is that something I do?

With a lion dozing fitfully a half-dozen spans from her, now was not the time. She kept one eye glued to the cat, but eventually the work was complete. At least to the best of her ability under the circumstances.

Now for the dangerous part.

She walked to the water side of the raft and pulled, gently at first, then harder when that didn't work. The raft made a loud scratching sound as it slid across the rock. The lion flinched, but didn't rise. She was starting to wonder if it ever would again. She had feared this beast from the moment she had seen its powerful tail lashing behind that rock formation. Looking at it now, it was hard not to pity the creature.

The raft stabilised in the water and floated better than she'd expected. She had to get her feet wet to reach its core, and so removed her boots before wading out to test her weight on it.

The raft held, and was even more steady than she'd expected. She climbed back off, pulling it back onto the beach just enough that it didn't float away.

There was one more thing she needed. Leaving the lion and raft behind, she headed up the shoreline in search of something she could use as a paddle. There were branches as far as the eye could see, but nothing broad and flat. In the end she was forced to make do with a misshapen tree root. She also grabbed another of the long, light logs as a backup, and returned to the raft. Taking care to place them without waking the lion, she headed around the debris pile to where she had buried the fishes to help keep them fresh. She uncovered and removed them from the hole before hearing a low growl.

Johanna's head snapped up as the lion lurched to its feet. It was unsteady, visibly swaying as it stood there, but it meant business. She looked at its weakened state, at its pure intent, and understood. The lion was a hair's breadth from its body failing entirely. It needed food if it was going to survive, and it needed it right now. It would spend its last breath attempting to do just that. She threw the vine-attached fish at it, unintentionally hitting the big cat in the nose as it stared her down. Whether it was luck, or the big cat's senses registering the smell, it abruptly lay down and consumed the first foot-long fish in a single bite. There was no gap between that and the second one, and Johanna moved. She headed around the debris again, encountering two more fish which she had ignored until now because she'd thought she had enough. She threw them at the lion as well. She could find food once she reached the garrison on the other island. It was time to leave. She picked up her boots and placed them on the raft before pushing it out into the water. The lion looked back at her for a moment, then decided they were done, and returned to its meal.

She picked up the broad, flat, tree root and began paddling, putting some distance between them before calling out on a whim.

"Sorry about the toes."

The lion ignored her. It had finished the meat and was lying curled up on its uninjured side.

Johanna nodded. Their time together was done.

She had expected to sit on the raft, but the water was smooth. For now at least she remained standing as she used the root to slowly paddle towards her goal.

The sun was falling through the sky, and she estimated another two, maybe three hours of usable light remained. Beyond that the island would become an inky blur indistinguishable in the darkness. She had to make it across before then, or she would likely drift off course and wake to an uninhibited horizon in every direction.

She kept paddling.

It was a beautiful day, there was a fresh ocean breeze, ample sunshine, and no more lion to worry about. How had it got out to this remote location in the first place?

One of the logs abruptly came loose from the raft, but she had tied each one separately, so it wasn't a disaster. Not yet. So long as the stabilising struts held and she could balance in the centre, she would be okay. Even so, she took a moment to remove her cloak and stuff it into her tunic. If the raft failed and she ended up in the water, it would drag too much for her to swim.

An hour later she was tired, hungry, and very thirsty. She hadn't particularly noticed it until now, but the ocean spray would occasionally brush her lips and remind her in detail that she had drunk nothing in over a day. The sun continued its dive from the heavens. She was barely halfway.

She kept paddling.

Another hour passed, and in her mind the day had turned from beautiful to monotonous. A stroke on the left, a stroke on the right to keep her in line. A stroke on the left…

The raft lurched, throwing her forward into the sea.

Johanna gasped as she scraped her face on something hard, and abruptly realised she wasn't in the water. She scrambled up onto her knees in confusion before realising that she was on the seabed. All around her the water level was dropping and a wave of fear engulfed her.

"Maker, no," she invoked, frantically stamping her feet into her boots. If yesterday's disaster had been any indication, she had less than a minute to reach the island before the wave hit.

She sprinted as fast as she could over the smooth rock of the ocean floor which the tsunami had scoured clean less than a day before. There was nothing but cliffs in front of her. Off to her right was a way up to safety, but it was a few hundred spans away. She would never make it in time. Feeling dread within her very soul, she kept glancing to her left for any sign the coming wave had begun to breach the ocean surface. She was almost to the island when she heard it. A great crashing, crunching roar that drowned out all other thought. It was coming fast. Far too fast to outrun or make it to the sloped access. The cliff in front of her was rough. One part in particular offered a natural chimney. She sprinted forward, heedless now of the smoothness of the seabed and any other thought than reaching the chimney. She didn't have to avoid the water completely, she just had to survive the impact without being carried into open water.

The wave reared up in the distance, ten foot high and moving at incredible speed, though it was nothing compared to yesterday's calamity. She reached the chimney first and shoved herself into the gap, clambering up as fast as she could while jamming her hands and feet against either side. The small, protected space had not been entirely cleansed by the tsunami, and enough handholds remained to help her gain some height.

The wave would be here in seconds. She wasn't high enough. Taking one more leap up the chimney she braced her hands, feet, legs and back as firmly against the walls of the chimney as she could.

The wave sped across the dry land, swallowing her raft in an instant. Then it slammed into her hiding space.

Everything begins somewhere.
Avsanian Saying.

CHAPTER 5

SURVIVOR

As the tsunami wave crushed her makeshift raft, Johanna took a deep breath, closed her eyes, and braced.

The impact tore her free of the crevasse, skinning her arms and legs as it sucked her out into the open water beyond. Thankfully the leading edge of the wave had moved fast enough that it passed her by instead of tumbling her along the seabed. As the wall of water reconquered the ground stolen from it for the second time in a day, it pulled her along in its wake instead.

Johanna tumbled through the surf, barely keeping her head above the churn as she swam desperately for a shoreline that was leaving her behind. The wave continued its headlong rush into the deeper water on the other side of the islands. Right now it was all she could do to stay afloat in the myriad of rips and currents which had formed as the incoming wave bounced off the surrounding islands.

The shoreline was getting more and more distant, and Johanna felt the stirrings of panic. Already she was several hundred spans north of the crevasse and the water was moving far too swiftly to swim against.

I'm being swept out to sea!

There was nothing for it but to try swimming around the

island. She couldn't compete with the wave's momentum. But if she could make it around to the sheltered northern beach, she might be enough in the island's shadow, so to speak, that the current wouldn't be so strong.

She began swimming with purpose. The hastily formed plan was all she had, and there was no backup. She swam for what seemed like ages, her skinned arms and legs adding to the list of hurts she had taken over the last two days. Was it her imagination, or was the water not quite so rough here?

Out of breath, Johanna took a moment to rest. She stopped her swim and treaded water to let her muscles and lungs recover. She glanced west to see how much further she had to go, and felt a deep stab of fear when she realised the large island was now to her south. A long way to her south. That was why the water was smoother and slower now, it had carried her into deeper water.

She fought the urge to dive straight back into another swim and instead forced herself to let her body recover. She was a strong swimmer, but she had to be half a mile from shore. A sprint would no longer do it. She looked back to the other islands and was forced to shield her eyes from a sun setting all too quickly. She had maybe an hour of light left. If she was still out here when it abandoned her, she would never find the island in the dark. Her heart raced again, and again she forced herself to calmness. Panic wouldn't save her any more than a flat-out sprint.

Once she had recovered her breath and her wits, she set out again with broad, sweeping stokes, swimming as efficiently as she knew how. An hour was plenty of time to swim a half mile, or even a full one. Her brain knew that. Her body wanted to rush, to go flat out, to reach safety in the shortest possible time. She shoved the impulse down mercilessly and kept going.

Eventually she looked up. She was closer to the island than before, but not nearly as close as she should be. The wave must still be pushing water across the land bridge that made up the islands, though nowhere near as strongly as before. She was winning, she just had to stay afloat and beat the weariness now creeping into her limbs, and the sun, to her destination.

All around her the tops of ripples were now glinting in the sunlight, and she returned to swimming. The ocean got dark at night. Even from her perch atop the plateau she'd had trouble making out the large island last night. From the surface, with the chop of the water, it might well be invisible. She swam on.

The sun plummeted towards the west, brushing the waves, then sinking beneath. There was still light, but it wouldn't last long. She could make out the beach now above the surf, but she was still two or three hundred spans from shore. Time was running out. The first stars were appearing above her, and while there was light to the west, she was already having trouble spotting the eastern horizon.

It was time for a sprint. If she could make it to the more sheltered waters behind the island, she could make it the rest of the way to shore. It was right in front of her, she could see where the wave pattern changed. A swirling current marked the narrow region where the tsunami waters still pushed gently north while the island provided a physical barrier to that current. Beyond it, the water appeared to be acting almost normally, waves heading in to shore, rather than away from it.

When she was perhaps fifty spans from the border, Johanna threw herself into the task. She was approaching exhaustion, but covered the distance. It wasn't until she reached the churning current that she realised her mistake. The water sucked her under instantly, and she struggled to make the surface. The lack of light didn't help, and for one confounding moment she didn't know which way was up or down. She let out a small bubble and watched it travel sideways before coming to her senses and reorienting herself. Swimming hard for the surface, she kicked for all she was worth and was tumbled again by the current. Panicking, she changed direction. The surface was only about three spans above her, and the current was manageable down here. The border with the island's water was thin. She made a choice and kicked and glided through the water as far as she could before heading back to the surface. She thought a quick prayer to the Maker as she rose. If she'd made it far enough, the current on the other side would aid, rather than hinder her. If she hadn't…

Lungs burning, she breached the surface and sucked in a half mouthful of air, half water as a wave smashed into her face. She began choking as she fought to stay afloat, but the light was fading fast. The waves had gone from clear to inky in a matter of minutes, and the eastern horizon was already lost to darkness. Coughing up water as she was spun around again, Johanna tried to gain her bearings. It was futile, the current had her, and it was all she could do to stay above the water line. She took in more water and spat most of it out, but couldn't stop coughing as some of it made its way into her lungs.

I have to get to shore, now!

She was about to set out in a random direction when the current abruptly released her. The glow of light on the eastern horizon was just a smear, and the stars were now out in force in a way that could rarely be seen from civilised lands. She couldn't see the island anymore, but she could make out a huge chunk of sky where those millions of stars were blanked out. It seemed the Maker had heard her. The churning current border had deposited her on its island side, but she still had to make it to shore.

Freezing cold, aching in every joint, and many places in between, she set out doggedly, aiming for that blank spot ahead. Her strength was all but gone, and she was still having trouble breathing due to the water she'd inhaled, but soon enough a wave grabbed her from behind. She'd reached the surf. She stopped swimming, exhausted, waiting for the next wave to come. She didn't have to wait long. Stiffening her body and making a closed V shape with her arms, she let the wave skim her in towards the shore as she'd done many times as a child.

I lived near the beach.

That was new.

It seemed her memories might come back in time after all.

Johanna smiled, but the expression turned to horror as the starlight reflected off a large rock right in front of her. She tried to drop off the wave, but it was too late. The darkness of night was replaced by that of a different kind as her head hit the implacable surface with a crunch.

*   *   *

Johanna woke in her own bed.

The sounds of a small bird chirping had disturbed her dream. She'd been swimming, or body-surfing, or something like that. It was already hazy. She swung her legs out from the covering sheet and stood after stretching. Today was an important day, the most important of her life, and she had to meet Joram at the octant by second tolling. The archmagi would not be impressed if she were late. Glancing at the window to make sure it was closed, she walked over and undid the latch on Fairy's cage. The brightly coloured little bird flitted up onto her shoulder.

The water bowl was almost empty, so using the Gift, she pulled some moisture out of the air and refilled it. There was still plenty of food, and that was harder to replace. She could do it when she returned home.

"There you go, Fairy."

The little bird chirped happily and flitted back to the cage to take a drink.

Leaving the bird to his own devices, she headed into the bathroom to take a shower. She turned on the taps and disrobed before the morning air could chill her too much. As soon as the water was warm enough, she stepped into the stream and sighed. The benefits of a modern city were not to be overlooked, and the new interconnected piping initiative was only in its infancy. She'd only had the house built last year though, and volunteered to be part of the trial. It was amazing to her that they could move all this water uphill without even needing the Gift. She'd cheated somewhat, helping to design a piece of arcana that mimicked the shape of the pipe and heated the water as it came through. The engineers had already placed an order with the College of the Arts for ten thousand more. It would be a lucrative contract for everybody involved.

Eventually every house would have the new infrastructure she supposed, but that would take many years. For now, she was just glad to have been in the right place at the right time to get in on the project early. After washing, she turned the taps off and used the Gift to dry herself. She went back to the bedroom, chose her clothes for the day and donned them. Black of course. That was a given because of her profession, though the choice of garment was her own. As always, a black cloak went over the top, its blue lining marking her at the rank of mage. If today went well, hopefully that would soon change. She'd long since fought her three battles on the western border, though battle magic wasn't her forte. She was still on the young side to be considered for the rank of Archmage, but it wasn't unheard of.

Trying to keep the smile off her face, she pulled on her boots and stopped to give Fairy a tickle under the chin before closing him back in his cage.

Leaving the house, she placed a ward across the door that would make it more secure than any lock. A mage could break it, but then, a mage could ignore the door altogether and blow a hole in the wall instead.

She was about to head for the octant when a small girl ran out of the neighbour's house in tears clutching a wooden horse that looked to have been beheaded.

"I hate you!" She screamed back at the house, and a woman standing in the doorway holding back a squalling toddler who had what looked to be the horse's head in his mouth.

"Janiah, come back inside. You know your brother didn't mean to knock your toy off the table."

"He's not a toy! He's Mr. Gallop!"

Johanna raised an eyebrow in vague amusement at the absolute sincerity in the small girl's voice and posture.

Taking a few steps towards the girl, Johanna looked down and said, "Maybe I can help with that."

The child noticed her standing there for the first time and went silent, looking up in awe as Johanna's shadow engulfed her.

She didn't run away, but she clearly didn't know what to make of a real live mage talking to her either.

Johanna knelt down, her cloak pooling around her.

"I'm Johanna, I live in the house next door. I'm sure you've seen me around."

Janiah nodded, all pretence of rage now gone.

A horse head came sailing down the few steps between them as the toddler threw it at his sister and hit Johanna in the knee. His mother chided him softly, not knowing how the mage who had moved in next door was going to take it.

Johanna just looked at the pair and gave them a grin.

"He has a good arm."

She could see the mother's shoulders relax, and gave them another smile before turning back to the girl. Janiah had taken the moment to pick up Mr. Gallop's head and clutch it to her chest.

"I could fix that if you like," she told the girl.

"Really?" Janiah replied. "Why would you do that for me?"

"Why not?"

Janiah didn't have a response to that logic, and hesitantly handed over the pieces of Mr. Gallop as though she were parting with a long sought-after treasure.

It was a moment's work to realign the head and body and use a wisp of the Gift to seal the line along which it

42

was cracked. The pieces of the wooden toy melded back into one.

Janiah snatched it out of her hands as soon as she was finished. Staring wide eyed at Mr. Gallop, she searched for any sign of the breakage, and of course found none.

"Thank you, Mage…" The girl said before realising she didn't know her name.

"Johanna," she supplied. But instead of using it, the little girl flung herself forward and gave her a tight but momentary hug before fleeing up the stairs, past her mother and back into the house.

"That was kind, Mage Johanna, my thanks," her mother said once she was inside.

"You're welcome. I have to go now, but I'm sure we'll meet again since we're neighbours now."

"That sounds nice. I'm Frieda by the way, and this is Stan," she said as she motioned at the toddler who had caused all this commotion.

"Pleased to meet you both," Johanna returned, before waving at the young boy and smiling when he stuck his tongue out at her. She returned the favour, and used the Gift to turn it bright green for an instant just for good measure. The boy laughed so hard he almost fell out of his mother's arms.

Frieda just stood there with a startled expression as Johanna walked away, her mind already turning back to the day's activities. She had a little time to spare before she needed to be at the octant, and a stroll through the bustle of the markets always took her mind off her worries.

It didn't take long to reach her destination, and the noises of the square sounded eerily familiar as turned the last corner.

A boy pulled a cart full of pies down the street, calling that his wares were two for a crown. Johanna frowned; she'd heard that before. Her head ached for no apparent reason, the pain growing until it forced her to sit, clutching her head as it began bleeding. She was just beginning to panic when the world went dark around her, and she slumped to the ground.

Assumption is at the root of every mistake. Or at least, so we assume.
Excerpt from 'Musings on Consciousness'.

CHAPTER 6

EXPECTATIONS

The ground was rough, and her head hurt. A lot.

Her arms were both grazed below the elbows, and her knees were a mess from the wave knocking her loose from the rock chimney a few hours before.

The cold wetness of a wave sloshed over her legs, and Johanna groaned as it all came back to her. The raft, the swim, the rock she'd ploughed into headfirst. Sadly, the rest of her life before waking on the island didn't re-emerge. This all might have been worth it if it had. She lifted her head. It seemed the surf had deposited her on the beach, undrowned and all. Johanna wasn't sure whether to thank it as she climbed to her feet. Apparently her left leg had hit the rock as well. She limped forward, testing her weight on the limb after feeling a large lump and bruise on its side. Nothing was broken, but she didn't remember ever having this many sore points on her body, ever. The last two days had been far from kind.

"Wait a minute!"

The dream she'd had while unconscious came rushing back in, causing her to stop in her tracks. She was a mage. They all were. All those bodies around her when she'd first woken, Joram and the others, they were all magi. She had been on her way to meet him. There had been something significant about that day, something they were going to do. Something they were going to reveal for the Archmagi from Miralthrall and Aramar. She'd had a part in inventing it.

She looked around. The hulking blackness of the island silhouetted the stars, creating a vast black mass in the night. But further up, there was a glow. It was faint, almost invisible, but just bright enough to illuminate the thin column of smoke rising away from it.

"There you are," Johanna muttered. All thoughts of the dream dissipated as the prospect of a warm fire, and maybe a meal and water, pushed to the forefront of her exhausted mind.

The light from the fire was significantly above her and to the south. Probably up on those same cliffs she'd seen it on last night from the other island. With any luck, she could find a slope gentle enough that she could make her way up there without having to climb.

She limped on her bad leg and took most of her weight with the right. Again and again, she shuffled forward. Off the beach with its stony sand, up a shallow hill bereft of all but the largest vegetation, and through a small thicket of trees which had escaped yesterday's disaster. There was little in the way of undergrowth, and she only stopped when she reached one of the sheer granite walls that seemed to permeate these islands. It was smooth and vertical. She couldn't have climbed it if she'd wanted.

She knew the garrison lay to the west, so she headed that way. Either she would find a way up to the higher elevations, or run into friendly troops. Using the stone to guide her through the darkness, she trudged her way across what turned out to be a large portion of the island. Eventually, the sheer wall ended, and she was able to make her way around and up its slope from the other side. If she was right, she could follow the far gentler edge back to where the campfire lay.

It had to be near midnight by the time she returned to where she'd first encountered the cliff. Only now she stood a hundred spans or more above the place she had occupied before. Smoke was rising from another thicket a few hundred spans south. Johanna sighed and kept walking. Her left leg felt like a piece of wood, and her head as though it were about to explode.

She moved through the trees, her body protesting with every step. What else could she do? To sit here, wet and freezing for another night, without hope of water in the morning might very well kill her after what she'd already been through. Even if it didn't, she suspected she would be too weak to continue.

The glow of fire promised salvation from that fate. It was all that drove her on.

For a long time it seemed she was making no headway, and then in the blink of an eye she was there, just outside the circle of light. She shook her head to clear it. She didn't think she had a concussion, maybe she was wrong?

She stumbled forward, taking little caution now that her target was within sight. The rosy glow of a fire peeked out at her from between the trees and she shuffled into the campsite before remembering to announce herself.

A dozen soldiers in leather armour jumped up, weapons in hand as she cleared the tree line. Others tried and failed; their wounds too severe. In an instant, unfriendly men surrounded her.

"Wait. The cloak! She's one of ours!"

The man nearest her took a better look, then smiled as if happy to see her. He sheathed his sword and rushed to her side to help support her weight.

I must look worse than I thought.

"Come on then, let's get you a spot near the fire. Looks like you've got a story to tell, Mage?"

"Johanna," she croaked.

The soldier supporting her motioned to another man, who threw a waterskin to him. She took it gratefully and gulped down the whole thing without thinking. The soldier who had passed it over gave her a sour look, which the man beside her saw.

"Doesn't matter Mick, now that we have a mage with us she can make all the fresh water we need."

"Go on then, we've been on stiff rations since the attack, and we've got a lot of men here who'd like to slake their thirst like you just did."

"Is that the way your mother taught you to ask for favours, Private?" The man beside her asked.

"My mother taught me to share. I did my part, beggin' the sergeant's pardon, but now it's time she did hers. We have wounded far more serious than that head knock she's taken."

The sergeant's lips thinned, but he didn't rebuke the man again.

"Look," he said to her instead. "You've obviously been through a bit, but my ill-mannered friend over here isn't wrong. Our injured could use more water than we have, both for drinking and cleaning their wounds. We'd be in your debt if you would make that happen."

Johanna just looked at him for a moment, and at all the

others waiting expectantly. Some had already gathered up pots and cups. These men thought she had come to save them…

She wanted to. She knew now that she was a mage, a good one at that. But right in this moment, she had absolutely no idea how to do what these men were asking of her. They would probably ask her to heal their companions' injuries next.

Suddenly, coming here didn't seem the best idea.

"Is that a problem?" the man beside her asked respectfully. She was still a mage, after all.

She still had those abilities, she realised, even as he waited for a response. The lion had proven it when she'd severed two of its toes. At the time, she hadn't understood, but now it made perfect sense. It had been a reflex action with no conscious thought behind it. She hadn't needed to recall how to cast that spell, and a spell was what it must have been. Something she'd practised regularly, something akin to the muscle memory of a well-practised fighter. Her memories seemed to be slowly returning. Perhaps the specifics of how to do these things would return in time as well? None of which helped her right now.

She looked at him and saw the expression turn sour on his face.

"I'm sorry. If I could, I would. I just don't know how."

"Well, that's just great. Thanks very much for drinking the last of our water! Are you even a mage?" Mick shouted.

"Enough!" the man beside her barked as Mick picked up a stone and threw it at her as hard as he could.

It should never have come near her if she really was a mage. She could have blown it up, vaporised it, melted or frozen it till it cracked, or just plain snagged it out of the air. As it was, her reaction times were dulled enough from hitting her head that all she could do was watch the stone abruptly expand to fill her field of vision. The projectile hit her squarely between the eyes.

As she faded towards unconsciousness yet again, Johanna could hear the two men talking over her.

"Tie her up," said Mick. "The captain can take care of her when she gets back."

"Suppose we don't have any choice. Wonder where she found the clothes?" The man who had helped her to the fire replied.

Best intentions aside, you should never have been there in the first place…
Excerpt from the court martial of General Jairus Mayweather after crossing the Wraith Woods against orders.

CHAPTER 7

AID FOR AID

The seating in the stadium was full.

Archmagi and Magi from both Aramar and Miralthrall were in attendance, and as she entered the octant, their voices quieted to nothing. Joram and the others were already waiting for her at their appointed places. This was her moment. She'd spent years on this research, ever since returning from the western border. It all came down to today.

She walked with forced calmness to a dais facing the crowd.

"Esteemed Archmagi and Magi, thank you for coming today, especially those of you who have travelled from across Jeranon to be here. Hopefully we can get you home a little quicker."

There was a smattering of laughter from the stands, but nothing too unruly. They all knew what they were here for. If it worked… When it worked, she cut herself off. It would change everything. From commerce, to war, to simple everyday travel, they would remake the world today.

She'd conducted small-scale tests on multiple occasions. She knew the spell worked. This time, the scale was just a little larger. Today she would attempt to send something all the way to Aramar. There was an identical octant built in the College grounds in the capital. If all went well, Archmage Inij would receive the package. After he had altered it in the prescribed manner, he would use the item of Gift-wrought arcana she had made for him to send it back. In theory, the entire display shouldn't take more than five minutes. It was what came next that would put her name in the history books…

She woke to the feel of rough ropes tied around her wrists, ankles, and torso. Beneath her was a sleeping roll, and on top, her blue-lined cloak was spread as a blanket. She was by the fire, which had reduced to a smoulder, By the look of it, the sun had risen some time ago.

"How was I supposed to know it would knock her out? She was wearing the uniform of a mage. I just wanted to rile her up enough to fill up the water skins. I never expected it would actually make contact," Mick implored.

"You'd better hope she doesn't hold a grudge," an unfamiliar voice warned. "And you. How did you let an unknown civilian drink the last of our water without challenge?"

"In my defence, Sir, I expected her to be capable of making as much as we needed once she recovered. Isn't that something that all of them can do?"

"It should be," the unfamiliar voice replied.

"She's awake," Mick said.

The conversation ended. Mick and the guard who had helped her came over to where she was struggling to sit up, accompanied by a short woman. Johanna's injuries and the ropes conspired to make the task near impossible.

"Let her go," the captain commanded after staring at her for a long moment.

"Captain…" Mick protested before the short woman cut him off.

"She's the real deal. I worked with her on the border a few years back. Not much of a battlemage, but her arcana was some of the best I've ever seen."

"Sir?" the nicer soldier enquired as he came over and began undoing the knots.

"Oh, you know. Arrows that explode on impact. Little glass balls that can generate a gust of wind strong enough to knock a tree down. Hardened swords that even the strongest Imbic mutation can't break."

"Impressive. Ever seen her pull water from the air?" Mick asked sarcastically.

"Actually, I have," the captain replied with a frown.

"Well, isn't that interesting," Mick commented.

"Go about your duties, Private."

"Mm hmm," Mick muttered as he walked away.

By the time Mick had left, the other soldier was freeing the last knot around her wrists. Johanna wasn't sure whether to thank the man or punch him.

"It's been a long time," the short terraliv woman wearing the insignia of a captain said by way of greeting.

Johanna frowned and nodded noncommittally as she refastened her cloak into position.

"You don't remember me?" the captain asked in surprise. "We spent two weeks together in that frozen hellhole up at Wyvern's Peak during the last invasion."

Johanna felt her mouth open, then close again when she came up blank.

"Well," the captain said, taken aback. "Even if you don't remember me, I certainly remember you. What's more is I'm going to have to insist you supply us with water. I've seen you do it before, Johanna."

Her mind turned furiously as she studied the captain. The woman had used her name, and it really was Johanna. The dreams *were* memories!

She sighed. Time to come clean.

"It's not so much that I don't remember you, Captain. It's more that I don't remember... me," she said. "I woke up two days ago on that island to the east, surrounded by the bodies of men and women wearing the same clothes I am dressed in. I have no memory before that point. Since then, I've just been trying to survive. I saw your fire last night and made my way here to look for help. I never imagined you'd need mine just as much."

"That's an understatement," the captain mused. "The army maintains a garrison of a hundred on this island to watch for western navel incursions, but the wave destroyed every fort and supply house they had."

Johanna's shoulders slumped. "So how do we get back to the mainland?"

"Maker knows," the captain invoked. "Look, Johanna, I'd love to catch up on old times, but as abrupt as Mick can be, he wasn't kidding. We need that water. All we had was what we were carrying two days ago, and the wave contaminated the only supply of fresh water on the island."

Johanna winced, remembering the waterskin she'd gulped down last night.

"I'm sorry. I can't."

"What do you mean you can't?" the captain interrupted. "I've seen you do it before!"

"I don't remember how," Johanna appealed. "You say I'm a mage, and I'm wearing these clothes, but I don't remember any of it! I didn't even know my own name until it came to me in a fragment of a dream. You knew that name, so I believe you when you say you know me, but I do not know who you are. And I certainly don't know how to cast that spell you want. Or any spell, for that matter. And also, I'd like to know what to call you."

The captain's eyebrows raised at her outburst, but her demeanour shrunk a little.

"You really don't remember?"

"Not even my own family. Wait, do I have a family?" she asked abruptly as the idea occurred to her.

"Two sisters, as far as I know, though I don't remember their names. Mine is Clarissa, though while we're on deployment, call me Captain Trelmaine."

"Thank you, Cl… Captain," Joahnna said in relief. She might have only been here a few days, but learning the captain's name, making that connection, was like a breath of fresh air after being stuck inside far too long.

"One more thing, we are on the Bulwark Islands, right?"

Again the eyebrow raise, though this time with a note of amusement behind it.

"Yeah, what's left of them. My men and I aren't even supposed to be here. We were part of a detached force hunting Imbic and Nostahl survivors on this island from a navel skirmish a week back. We were on patrol on higher ground when the first wave hit. Lucky us. After it subsided, we set up camp here to tend to the wounded. I went to get help from the garrison, but the entire area was scoured clean by the ocean. If there are survivors on this island beyond what you see in our camp, we haven't encountered them."

"What about the westerners?"

"Haven't seen them since the wave either. With any luck, that tsunami did our job for us. It better have. I've got less than a dozen combat ready men. We tracked and killed two Imbic before the wave hit, and think they were the only two to make it to shore since we have seen no other tracks…"

"But it's a big island," Johanna finished.

"Yep," Trelmaine confirmed.

"So what do we do now?" Johanna asked, afraid the answer was going to be that there was nothing they could do.

"We're going to last as long as we can and hope for rescue. Provided the docks at Northwatch weren't destroyed, they'll be sending someone to check on the garrison after that wave hits the mainland. In the meantime, I'm going to continue patrolling for westerners. Your only task now is to work out how to cast that water spell, or any other that will give us something to drink. Keep us alive long enough for the relief vessel to get here, and I'll make sure it transports you back to the mainland…"

"You feel it too?" Johanna asked, the fear rising in her like a wave. Clarissa nodded.

"Brace!" Trelmaine called to her men as the ground began to vibrate.

All around them men sat or rushed to stabilise their injured comrades. A few seconds later, the trembling ended as abruptly as it had begun. The sudden cessation leaving everyone looking around in confusion, waiting for the other shoe to drop.

Trelmaine remained standing. She nodded to the quiet

soldier, and he took off at a jog towards the eastern cliff.

"Only a small one, quit sitting around!" She announced with bravado.

Some of the men laughed, but it was forced and humourless.

An hour later, the soldier returned.

"Report, Millard," Trelmaine ordered as soon as he was in range.

"No wave. A rolling surge, but that's all. They're getting smaller each time."

Trelmaine nodded, her relief palpable in the movement.

"Alright. Millard, Mick, Aterby, you're with me. Johanna, work on that spell," Trelmaine said without preamble, then set off to the east with the others in tow.

There is nothing more dangerous than an unfocused mage.
Excerpt from 'The Gift'.

CHAPTER 8

EXPERIMENTATION

Johanna was a mage.

She had been told multiple times. She was dressed in their uniform, and what few memories she had, agreed.

Two days had passed since she'd reached their fire, and things were looking grim. Five of the injured men had already passed into the Black Lady's embrace, and tempers were fraying as those remaining progressively moved towards delirium from lack of water. Trelmaine hadn't gone on patrol today, and even Mick was quiet, napping, or possibly unconscious on his sleeping roll.

She had to figure this out. Of them all, she was in the best condition, having finished the last of their water when she'd arrived. She couldn't help but feel guilty over that. After two days without water, the soldiers were now in nearly the same condition she'd been in when she'd stumbled into their camp.

The others had given her what advice they could, sharing their limited knowledge of the Gift. Trelmaine had been a little more helpful, having worked with magi directly in the past, but even her mantra of visualise, clarify, intend, hadn't helped. It was like being told you could fly. That you'd been able to your whole life. That you'd just forgotten how. Her brain couldn't quite bring itself to accept the notion. She was beginning to suspect that was the problem. How could her imagination create something when her intellect didn't believe she could succeed?

At least they had plenty of food. Aterby had brought down one of the garrison's sheep with his bow yesterday. None of them knew how the animal had survived the waves. None of them had cared. Their bellies were full, though it was no substitute at all for a full skin of water.

Trelmaine had talked about pulling water out of the air, but how did you go about doing that? It was just there. You couldn't see it, touch it, or taste it. On a hot day, you could feel your clothes get damp from the humidity, so you knew it was there. Knowing it was there didn't help her translate that moisture into liquid inside a cup for someone to drink. She sighed. She was missing something, some vital aspect of spell casting that made the whole thing work. If she couldn't figure it out, that one step would be the death of them all, and not in some nebulous future. Some of these men were already at breaking point, having been on tight rations even before the water ran out. Some were injured, and weaker than they should have been to start with. Another day would see half of them dead. Two more and there would be almost no one left. In three, even her body would fail. From the conversations she'd had with Clarissa over the last two days, Johanna now knew it took years to train a mage the first time around. How was she supposed to relearn this specific skill in time, and without a proper teacher?

She held a metal cup in her hand. It was the lightweight, hardy kind that soldiers kept in their packs on extended patrols. For two days now she had been attempting to fill it, to no avail.

She had tried imagining water filling the cup in every way possible, but every time she looked, the only contents were air. The crucial piece of the puzzle had to be somewhere in her mind. She had been hoping to find it in her dreams, as she had her name, and the fact that she was a mage. But all she kept dreaming of was that day in the octant. What had she been doing? What had she been about to reveal, and why was it so important to her?

She thought back to the memory of fixing Janiah's toy horse. What had she done there? How had she made that spell work?

She closed her eyes and tried to remember. She watched in her mind's eye as the wood grain seamlessly came together, not glued, but fused back into a single piece. That didn't matter. How had she made the spell activate?

'Imagine your target how it is,' a vaguely familiar voice whispered in her mind.

She sat up straight. Had that been a memory? If it was, it was the first waking recall she'd had since coming to these islands.

'Now, imagine what you want it to be. Anyone can do this, yes?' the voice continued.

Johanna sat stock still, doing her best to block out the rest of the world and let the memory flow.

'The job of a mage is to use the Gift to change what we call reality from one to the other.'

Johanna felt something within her mind… shift, and startled as a fat drop of rain hit her. It was followed by thousands more as a torrent cascaded down out of a clear blue sky.

Startled exclamations sounded from all around, and those men still with the presence of mind to, began rummaging through packs in search of containers to capture the sudden deluge. Within seconds they were all saturated, though twenty spans in any direction the ground was dry. Injured men lay prone with mouths open to slake their thirst, and Trelmaine was uncovering cook pots and turning their lids upside down.

The captain looked over at her and nodded in sincere thanks as all around them men stood with mouths opening and closing towards the sky as they swallowed mouthfuls of rain. It was a bizarre sight, almost like they were praying.

Something unexpected had happened in her mind right before the deluge, something not borne of conscious thought.

It can't be that simple.

For days, she had been imagining water filling her little cup, imagining it overflowing, imagining the sweet, clear liquid coming from any number of sources, and nothing had happened. Could it really be that she had just been imagining those things without actually doing anything about it? A Giftless child could have done as much. The rain stopped as abruptly as it began, and Johanna looked down to see her cup was full to the brim. Not overflowing, and not half a finger width of empty room inside.

It was what she had envisioned, though at no point had she intended it to rain. Clearly she had a long way to go in regaining her skills, but this would do for a start.

The men were already drinking from their cups when Johanna realised she didn't know how to make this happen again.

"Wait!" she called urgently, halting some, but not others.

"Listen up!" Trelmaine called with more authority than Joahnna had ever used in her life.

The men paused and looked at her, though only years of habitually following orders had made them halt.

"You need to save as much of that water as you can. Right now I have no idea how I did this, and I don't know when, or even if, I'll be able to do it again."

Several of the men's shoulders slumped, but Trelmaine's voice rang out over their disappointment.

"Righto, you heard what Mage Johanna said! Pour whatever you've collected into the pot and make sure the wounded have their share. After that we clean and bathe their wounds and then ration whatever's left."

Reminding them of their wounded comrades' needs seemed to do the trick, and while there were a few grimaces as men poured their coveted water into the main pot, nobody complained.

"Millard, Aterby, see the wounded get what they need. Mick, take two men and do a half mile patrol, make sure our perimeter is secure. Johanna, I could use your help to change their dressings."

Mick saluted and left, and Johanna found herself obeying as well. Captain Trelmaine ran a tight ship.

As it turned out, cleaning the injured men's wounds was little more than removing bandages made of uniform scraps and checking to make sure infection hadn't taken hold. With no supplies to speak of, there wasn't much more they could do. The first man they tended had a nasty gash down his thigh, but the wound had been cleaned and sewn when it had first occurred. He seemed weak, but on his way to recovery. Using a bowl from someone's pack, Trelmaine took an inch of water from the pot and used the precious liquid to clean around the wound.

"Don't suppose you could help with this?" the captain asked.

Johanna just shook her head. "I don't dare. I was only trying to fill my cup before, and I set off a deluge. If something like that happened while I was working on their flesh…"

Trelmaine nodded. "I take your point. Bring the water," she said.

They moved on to the next soldier. Once his bandages were removed, they revealed a shocking series of puncture wounds around his upper and lower legs. The man wouldn't be walking anytime soon, if ever again.

Johanna glanced at Trelmaine, horror clear on her face. "What?"

"Nostahl…" the captain bitterly replied. "If you see one, kill it before it kills you. Or does something worse."

Johanna could only nod in response. There must be thirty or forty hastily sewn up stab wounds here. How had the man not bled out?

A shudder ran through the man's body as they tended him. Despite being unconscious, he could clearly feel the pain even now.

Others were in similar conditions, some better off, some worse. Few of them would ever leave this spot without assistance. As they moved down the line, uniforms were torn, and the scraps used as newer bandages. By the time they finished, the men looked more like a desperate band of beggars than a unit of the king's rangers.

Once the distasteful task was complete, Trelmaine

motioned for one of the able-bodied men to stow the equipment before taking her aside.

"Eventually, we're going to need to move these men down to the beach. I don't suppose you could rig up some of those stretchers you made for us up at Wyvern's Peak? The ones that used a cushion of air to glide just above the ground?"

"Sorry, I don't remember those," Johanna told her with genuine regret.

"I figured," Trelmaine replied. "Had to ask though. It's going to be tough getting all these wounded down there. There just aren't enough of us in a condition to haul them to the beach in one trip. To say nothing of guarding them at either end."

"Can't we just wait up here until help arrives?"

"Right now, we don't even know if help is coming. If the wave didn't make it as far as the mainland, they may not even know we're in trouble. From what I understand, the next supply run should be in four days' time. If they sail up and see the garrison washed away without spotting survivors, they'll turn around, sail home, and report. If that happens, we'll be stuck here for good, or at least for long enough that it won't matter when they come back. Of course, if they do know we're in trouble, that ship could come anytime. We need to be ready."

"There's something you haven't told me yet though, isn't there," Johanna prompted when the captain fell silent.

Trelmaine looked up at her with a frown.

"We're only here because of a serious western incursion. When my unit detached from the ship carrying us, the western fleet was still largely intact. There may not be a spare ship to send right now. If the rest of the battle went poorly, there may not be any ships to send at all."

"Then we'll have to fend for ourselves," Johanna replied. "We can best feed ourselves at the shoreline, and I'll work out this water supply issue, somehow."

Trelmaine nodded. "Hope for the best, prepare for the worst."

"Sounds like a plan," Johanna said.

Trelmaine smiled, then lost the expression before turning back to her men.

"Listen up, here's what we're going to do."

CHAPTER 9

MORE VALUABLE THAN GOLD

After her little rainstorm, the rest of the previous day had been spent rigging up enough stretchers to carry the injured down to beach. With the tremors becoming less and less violent, Trelmaine thought it was safe enough now to leave the rocky outcropping they'd been camped on for the last several days. They needed to be where they would know when a rescue ship had arrived. That meant the docks, or at least, where the docks had been.

The night had been cold, the fire barely sufficient to ward off the chill, but morning had come at last.

It was time.

Trelmaine walked into the middle of the campsite and demanded their attention.

"Today I want the camp shifted beachside. We don't know when a rescue or resupply ship will come, but it is imperative that we are ready to signal it when it does. There are more injured than we can carry in one trip, so Mick, Millard, you'll stay behind. Stow the remaining gear and guard those who'll need to wait for the second or third trip."

"Yes, Ma'am," Mick replied, while Millard nodded.

"Good. Everyone else, pair up and take a stretcher, let's move out."

Johanna paired up with Aterby while Trelmaine scouted the way ahead. It had taken her some time to make her way around the cliff and up here after she'd survived the swim from the other island. The western shore would be further still. Adjusting her grip on the heavy stretcher, she settled in for a long walk as Aterby led them after Trelmaine.

Soon enough they were back at the cliff, and the view of the ocean reflecting the morning sun like a million sparking diamonds filtered through trees which grew increasingly sparse. A light breeze brushed across her neck as they walked, and aside from the grimness of their situation, the islands were quite beautiful, she thought, if a little cold.

The soldier behind her cursed, tripping on a rock, but not losing hold of his stretcher. The man got back to his feet, looking more embarrassed than hurt, and the procession continued. For a long time there was an almost eerie quiet; the only sounds the laboured breathing of soldiers and now and then, a random gust of wind. She was coming to realise that there was very little in the way of animal life on the islands, especially after the wave had scoured most of their coastlines. Not for the first time, she wondered how the lion had made it all the way out here, so far from its natural mainland habitat. With an odd pang of regret, she realised she hadn't thought about the creature since the moment her raft had bottomed out on the way here. Had it survived the second wave? She was forced to acknowledge that it almost certainly hadn't. The beast had been in awful shape when she'd left, and there hadn't been long between then and when the aftershock had hit. In a strange way, the enormous feline had been the first creature she'd ever seen. Now that a stretch of ocean safely separated them, she could admit that she would be sorry if the magnificent beast were gone.

After what seemed like hours, Johanna's arms felt like they were weights tied to the stretcher, and not appendages at all. She stumbled forward as Aterby stopped without warning, and joined him in lowering the stretcher as he crouched.

Ahead of them on the path, Trelmaine was signalling them to get down, and Johanna copied Aterby's stance. Behind them, the others did the same as Trelmaine returned to the column in haste.

"We've got problems," she hissed as she reached them. "About two hundred spans ahead, there is a rock formation. Behind it is a camp full of Nostahl. Aterby, get back to camp and retrieve Mick and Millard. We're going to need them."

The man nodded and was off, crouching as he ran back the way they'd just come.

"With me, and stay quiet," Trelmaine said as she motioned Johanna to follow.

Johanna frowned. Why her and not one of the other soldiers? There was no time to think about it though. Trelmaine was already moving ahead, expecting her to follow.

Trelmaine noticed her hesitation and slowed just long enough for her to catch up. The two women crouched as they approached the rock formation. Johanna's heart was racing by the time they were a hundred spans from it, pounding once the distance was only fifty.

Why am I doing this?

Trelmaine slowed, moving sideways towards a large thicket of foliage. She crouched even lower and crawled inside, forcing Johanna to follow.

Down on her hands and knees now, Johanna crawled after the captain for several spans until they came to a natural break in the rock formation ahead.

Still obscured by the foliage, she could see maybe two dozen short, grey, leathery skinned creatures manning the camp. Most were around three feet high, none taller than four, and each sported a pair of shiny, black, nub-like horns sprouting from their head, like that of a young goat. Many bore the mark of wounds, though all appeared mobile, unlike Trelmaine's forces.

Remembering the violent assault on the legs of the soldier they'd first treated; she doubted their version of healing involved caring for those of their number too injured to move.

"What do you think?" Trelmaine whispered beside her.

Johanna frowned. Surely the captain couldn't be thinking about attacking this camp? The western troops outnumbered them two to one. Then she saw it.

Across the camp, a short Nostahl was taking a clawed handful of water from a large barrel, and not having to reach too far to get it. There were also several wooden crates nearby, unopened, and likely full of supplies. A few were even marked with the king's seal, and had likely washed up onshore after the first wave. No matter what argument she made, Johanna knew Trelmaine would want those supplies.

"What do you think our chances are of winning?" she whispered back.

Clarissa gave her a sideways glance and grimaced. "It's a very even fight. If we maintain and make use of the element of surprise, we should be able to open well and gain the advantage."

"And if our plan doesn't go the way we expect?"

"We'll be in trouble," the captain admitted. "But without knowing when or even if a rescue is coming, we need those supplies. Even if we have to fight to get them. Not to mention that eliminating this very group was my detachment's primary mission before all this came down."

After watching for a few more minutes, Trelmaine motioned for her to back up. There wasn't room to turn around, so they crawled backwards the way they had come, doing everything possible not to get her cloak caught, or shake the branches as they moved. After clearing the thicket, Trelmaine glanced towards the camp to make sure nothing had changed. With a nod saying they were good to go, they dashed back to where the rest of the men were waiting out of sight.

The next quarter hour passed slowly, and Trelmaine ordered the stretchered soldiers be moved further off the path. Once done, she filled the others in on what they'd seen while they waited for the three missing men to arrive.

Aterby appeared first, followed by Mick and Millard, who joined the able-bodied soldiers at the front of the column.

"All right, here's the situation. By best count I make twenty-two Nostahl beyond the rock formation ahead. They have in their possession a large supply of water and several crates from the garrison's supplies. We're going to liberate those supplies and complete our mission here in one fell swoop, but we'll have to be careful. Their numbers balance our own. Most of us are banged up and won't be fighting at our best. Fortunately, they don't seem to have fared any better, so again things even out."

There were nods all around, even some grins. After the overwhelming helplessness of the last few days, these men were ready for a fight. They were eager for something they could control, and knew how to do well.

"Mick," Trelmaine continued. "You're our fastest runner, so you get to be the decoy."

"Lovely," the private commented, though seeming undeterred.

"You'll 'stumble' onto their camp and then retreat around the rocks to where the rest of us will be waiting. Johanna and Millard, you'll be furthest around the rock formation at our rear. I want you there to scare the living daylights out of any Nostahl that thinks its clever enough to flank us."

"Wait a minute! You understand that I'm basically a civilian until the rest of my memories come back, right?" Johanna protested.

"That's why Millard will be there. Only a few should come your way, and you'll scare and distract them with your mage's uniform. He'll kill them.

"Oh, okay..." Johanna replied, but the captain had already moved on.

"Aterby, take up position fifty spans from the rocks and keep a line of sight to fire on any Nostahl that gets past us and continues after Mick. Once you two are clear, join the fray."

She looked around at the assembled soldiers. "Get this right and its campfires, good food, and beach sunsets until the ship comes in. Everybody clear on their tasks?"

There were nods all around, and a few quiet 'yes ma'am's'.

"Alright, absolute silence until we spring the trap."

She stood and headed straight for the rock with the others close behind.

It was hard to sneak in a group, but they managed it, approaching the rock formation without being spotted.

Johanna took her place at Millard's shoulder. She raised a hand in a manner she imagined looked as though she were about to cast a spell, and did her best to look imposing. She felt like an idiot, and a scared one at that.

The moment they were all in position, Trelmaine nodded.

Mick began his approach.

The bigger they are, the harder they hit.
Terraliv saying.

CHAPTER 10

CAMPFIRES AND SUNSETS

Mick winked as he passed their position, sauntering on past as if he had not a care in the world. A moment later he moved within sight of the enemy camp and yelled in mock surprise.

The man sprinted back past them without looking in their direction, and an instant later, the pounding of footsteps sounded from behind the rock. Johanna watched as Trelmaine counted to three and then reached out to snag the first Nostahl to clear the rock. She flung the creature towards the rest of them, and it went down immediately.

Johanna heard footsteps on her side of the rock and Millard nodded for her to be ready.

The short creature rushed headlong at them, recoiling when it saw her mage's cloak and upraised hand. Millard took a step forward and calmly thrust it through with his blade. Two more appeared right afterwards, but Clarissa had been right, just the sight of her was enough to make them hesitate. Millard had no problem dispatching them all.

Behind them a pained shout rang out and then cut off. Millard turned and joined the fight, leaving her alone for the moment. There were no more footfalls, so she turned as well and raised her hands again.

It was enough that several of the Nostahl turned to charge her, and she knew she'd made a mistake. She backed off whilst struggling to maintain her 'ready to cast' appearance, and an arrow took the lead creature in the eye, dropping it in its tracks.

A moment later Mick was charging into the group, and they stopped following her as they turned to face the more immediate threat. She startled as she backed into something. A tree. A tree that moved. With a sick sensation she turned to look. It wasn't a tree. It was a leg. She looked up in horror at the Imbic mutation. It was massive, at least six spans high. The leg she had bumped into had three feet attached at various points along its length. Its other leg was shrivelled and only half as long.

Every Imbic was physically different from the rest. This one had a massive arm on the side of the shrivelled leg, and a head that protruded from its chest at right angles to the sky. Where its other arm should have been was a lumpy protuberance with no useful limb attached. Whether the result of an injury, or simply how this mutation had been born was anybody's guess. Not that it mattered as it swung its vast appendage and grabbed her as though she were a toy.

The creature looked at her for an instant before throwing her clear over the rock formation and into the enemy camp.

As she reached the top of the arc and plummeted towards the ground with horrifying speed, terror gripped her. For a moment she couldn't breathe. She hit the ground hard and bounced, scraping along the packed dirt where she landed. The world spun as she tumbled again and again until finally it stopped, or she did. It was hard to tell.

Johanna groaned. Every part of her ached or burned or

worse, and she was pretty sure her left arm was broken.

There was an inhuman scream from somewhere nearby and she forced herself to raise her head.

The mutation was coming.

She tried to stand, and collapsed again as her ankle gave out. Was that broken as well? The Imbic loped towards her on its good hand and leg. It was coming for her, and she couldn't move fast enough to get away.

An arrow sprouted from its head, though it paid little attention. Another shaft pierced its right eye. The thing screamed, but kept coming. It reared up over her, a monster the size of a boulder. As it brought its enormous fist slamming down at her, she knew this was the end.

Something in her mind clicked.

An instant before the mutation could kill her, a blue glow appeared all around in a sphere that took the impact of the blow, leaving her dazed, but unharmed.

The thing tried again, taking still more arrows every few seconds. They might as well have been toothpicks apart from the one in its eye. Again it slammed its fist into her shield, this time hard enough to push her sideways. Two of the soldiers had reached it now and were hacking at its massive leg. The thing must have had thicker skin than normal though, and the soldiers were annoying it more than anything else. It put its hand on the ground and kicked out, crushing one of the men against the rock formation. The other darted back to help with the remaining Nostahl, recognising how badly over-matched he was until help could arrive.

The mutation turned its attention back to her, this time trying something new. It set itself on its good leg and scooped up her entire shield bubble in its one massive hand, Johanna still inside.

"No, no, no, no, no!" Johanna squealed as it wound up and smashed her against the rock formation. The shield held. Barely. But the force was enough to fling her against its edge, seriously jolting her injured arm and back.

The horror remained unsatisfied, and pulled her shield back again. She couldn't take another of those impacts.

The thing didn't care. It wanted to do her harm. Johanna's heart ceased as the thing smashed her against the rock wall again. Her shield buckled and vanished in an instant, surviving just long enough to halt the massive hand's momentum. Gravity embraced her, and she fell between the mutation's now-still fingers and the rock. She landed hard, though it was nothing compared to the force of the Imbic's blows, and felt herself curl up into a ball.

The creature wasn't finished with her though, and reached down with two massive fingers to take hold of her hair. She screamed as it lifted her off the ground and up to the level of its face. It smiled at her with half a mouth of perfect teeth, and half a mouth of serrated bone that might have belonged on a shark. The thing opened its span-wide mouth, and Johanna suddenly understood what it intended. Horrified, something shifted in her mind, and without warning, the Imbic's entire body exploded in a mountain of gore. She dropped to the ground in a pile of viscera, landing on an already broken arm as the world went black.

*　　*　　*

She looked out over a frozen bluff. Below her an army searched for a way past their defences. There wasn't one.

Wyvern's Peak was built here for just that reason.

Over centuries, the men and women stationed here had dug and carved, used the Gift and prepared for an attack just like this.

It was finally happening. The western nations had been stupid enough to try sending a force over the apex of the Dark Iron Mountains.

If it had worked, they would have entered Jeranon though a region of the mountains that avoided Stonekeep's defences. They would have lost many soldiers to accomplish it, but they might have considered the sacrifice worthwhile if they caught the Jeranonian army off guard.

"Are the traps ready?" She heard herself ask.

"We're about to find out," Trelmaine answered, her uniform proclaiming her a sergeant.

Johanna looked down at the mass of bodies moving up the channels towards them. From the enemy perspective they were just natural divots and crevasses in the mountain's topography. Years of snow and detritus hid their true nature, except from above.

"Blow the horn," Johanna ordered.

Trelmaine used a small stick to light the end of an indicator, then threw it out the window. In seconds, the Gift-wrought object had caught fire and was spewing a thick red smoke that would be visible for miles.

Seconds later a horn sounded in the distance. It was a vast sound, deep, and felt more than heard. It rang out again, and again, until an ear shattering crack accompanied its final blast. There was a tremendous gust of wind as all the air was momentarily sucked out of the room, causing every flame to stutter and die.

Johanna took a step forward and looked out the window. Below her, entire enemy regiments were fleeing ahead of a wall of snow dislodged by the vibrations from the horn. She could hear their screams as the Nostahl, Augrahl, and even a few Imbic were buried, or dislodged from the mountainside to be carried towards their doom.

The avalanche was unforgiving, yet hundreds of the enemy survived, perhaps thousands. When it was safe, they gave a cheer at still being alive. They didn't know what else was waiting for them.

Trelmaine turned to her and grinned. "They seem eager. Shall I get the next stage ready?"

"Please do," Johanna replied. "Let's put the channels to use next."

"I was hoping you would say that," Trelmaine answered.

*　　*　　*

When she came to, someone was washing her arm with a sponge of all things.

Millard smiled as he saw she was awake, and put a gentle hand on her shoulder to keep her where she was.

"Don't move," he insisted. "There are more parts of you injured than not."

She tried to nod, sending a sharp pain down her spine at the movement, slight though it was.

"We won?" She managed through parched lips. She must have been here for a while.

"We eliminated the enemy. In no small part thanks to you," he said.

"You don't seem happy about that," she replied. "What happened?"

He looked away with a frown and pursed lips, as if unsure how much to tell her.

"Before it followed you into the camp, the Imbic took a swing at us, scattering our formation. Between the men it killed outright, and the Nostahl taking advantage of us being separated, we lost seven men. And the captain."

Johanna felt tears spring to her eyes. The terraliv woman had protected her, given her purpose and hope when she had none, and now she was gone.

"Yeah," Millard agreed, going back to cleaning a scrape that ran from her shoulder to elbow. One of many. It hurt, but right now she didn't care. If only she could control these powers, she could have saved them all. She had encountered the Imbic first. She could have dealt with it then...

"Hey, none of that now. I know that look and it wasn't your fault. None of us knew that monster was lurking nearby, and the captain never would have ordered an assault if she had. In fact if it wasn't for what you did, that thing would have turned around and come for the rest of us next. If your mind must focus on a detail, make it that one."

Some of the tension went out of her shoulders, the movement hurting in places she didn't expect. Her left arm was now bound with a proper bandage and immobilised against her chest. Most of her clothes had been removed so they could tend to her wounds, but they had placed an actual blanket both over and under her for comfort and privacy.

"How long have I been out?" She asked urgently, though abruptly wondering why it mattered.

"A day and change. Long enough that I was becoming

worried you weren't coming back to us. I think your arm is cracked below the elbow, but I'm not a medic. We'll have to see how it goes in a few days."

"Are we still in danger?"

He shook his head. "I don't think so. We accounted for all the Nostahl during the fight, and our patrols have found no tracks outside the immediate area. As far as we can tell, we got them all."

Johanna nodded, not feeling much of anything at the news.

"I think I'm going to sleep now," she said instead.

"Wait a minute," Millard insisted, reaching over and filling a cup with some clean water before helping prop her head up so she could drink it.

When she was done, she mumbled her thanks, and was asleep before he'd even removed his hand.

CHAPTER II

THE MOUNTAIN PATH

Johanna looked up at the overly large classroom where she sat in the second row at her normal desk.

Archmage Exmarl looked down at her work, frowning in concentration as she attempted to decipher what she called Johanna's 'spider's-crawl' writing.

Johanna didn't see what was wrong with it, and that annoyed the archmage to no end.

"That's correct, Johanna," the elderly woman approved, moving on.

Archmage Exmarl was their instructor for today, and was busy testing them on the foundational theories of magic. It was sooooo boring.

She'd only been at the College for six phases now, and these kinds of tests were becoming wearisome. When were they going to do some real magic?

Her parents had moved to the city so she could still live with them instead of sending her here to study like so many other future magi. But right now, all she wanted was to be home. Her real home back in Pereset, the one that was a short walk from where her friends lived. Not the townhouse they had here. It was a pleasant house to be sure, far nicer than their old home in fact. Even after all these phases though, it felt sterile, empty of all the most important connections one associated with a proper home.

She looked down at the words she'd scrawled on her page. Imagination, focus, execution. The three critical steps to casting any spell.

Johanna's eyes flew open. An unfamiliar palm tree shaded her.

She was on a sleeping roll, the ground beneath her was granite, and a litter like the ones they'd made for the injured soldiers lay beside her. Mick lay on it, his left arm bandaged and bloody from shoulder to wrist. The gruff soldier slumbered fitfully. She rolled to her side, every muscle aching, though somehow she seemed more or less intact as she reacted instinctually. She ran a finger lightly down the bandage, and the material sliced away as if her finger were a blade.

Almost like magic, she thought with a small grin. She was too sore to rise, but she could reach him from here.

Not daring to stop and think about what she was doing, she peeled the bandage away, and a powerful sensation of familiarity overcame her. She'd done this before. Many times, if she guessed correctly. With the ageing bandage out of the way, she saw a blade had sliced along the man's limb almost its entire length, stopping just short of the veins on his wrist. She placed her hand across the top of the wound at the narrowest point and wondered what to do next.

A strange blue glow emanated from her palm, and she felt an awareness of the wound that transcended physical sight. In an instant she could feel every contour of broken flesh, every blood vessel, every damaged muscle and ligament, even the shallow scoring along the bone. But what to do next. A flash of panic took hold as she realised her instincts had brought her this far, but would take her no further.

Why had she been so sure she could do this? The dreams had to be the key... They were all she knew.

She closed her eyes, ignoring her physical senses as she studied the wound more closely with the delving spell. Yes, that was what it was called! Johanna smiled. Perhaps her memories were closer to returning than she'd thought? But what was the next step? She felt as though she were close to the answer.

Imagination, focus, execution.

The three words floated to the top of her mind. The foundational theories of magic. Execution, she thought she understood.

When she'd drenched them all back at the cliff side camp, she'd felt something move in her mind, something like the tumblers in a good lock falling into place. She'd accessed something, *done* something, not just imagined it happening like a child might have.

Imagination seemed obvious. She couldn't cast a spell if she couldn't picture in her mind what she wanted to happen. But what was focus? It had to differ from imagination, but how?

The image of Mr. Gallop flashed through her mind, and she frowned. How was that related? Her subconscious seemed to be leading her somewhere, and she was more than willing to follow. But what did a wooden horse have to do with the foundational theories of magic?

She thought back on that dream, the images, for now, still clear and sharp. She'd taken the toy from Janiah and examined it, feeling the grain along the broken pieces. Then she'd placed them together and done something. Not glued or fused them, something else, something more like returning the component parts to their natural order. In the dream, she examined the edges of the toy, trying to focus on the moment she'd cast the spell. Johanna watched herself meld the toy into one piece, but it wasn't clear how. She tried focusing on the toy itself, replaying the scene again in her mind. Johanna could almost see what was happening this time. She imagined herself even closer, and watched in fascination as the two halves of Mr. Gallop came back together. The spell she cast didn't fix the toy in the traditional sense. The pieces were now one piece, just as every other part of the wood which hadn't been broken was one piece, and had been all along. Once the spell was complete, there was no longer a point of weakness, no longer a point of breakage. It was whole once again.

Johanna's eyes flew open as she felt flesh knitting back together along the portion of Mick's wound under her hand. She concentrated on the delving spell, making sure each blood vessel, muscle, and ligament found its proper place before melding them back to the other side of the wound.

She must have been working on it for an hour when she noticed Mick was awake. The man was staring at her, barely breathing, trying to control the pain without interrupting her spell.

"Thank you," he said as she noticed his stare.

She nodded slightly before returning her concentration to his wound. Most of it was healed now. The section where she'd worked was closed and whole without even a scar. It was unnatural, and yet, that was the point. She was using the Gift, and this time it was working the way she intended!

She went back to the wound, but her focus was waning, the small amount of energy she'd recovered since the attack now spent. Her head spun, but she pushed on, determined to at least do this before she passed out again. Maybe that Imbic mutation had done more damage than she'd thought.

She did her best to abandon her natural senses and only concentrate on what she was doing with the Gift, but it was becoming increasingly difficult to concentrate. A wave of vertigo made her want to retch.

"It's okay," a voice reached her, even in that state. Mick's. "I'll be all right, rest."

She ignored the voice and kept going, returning the last of the severed flesh back to its natural state as one undivided piece.

The moment she was done, a sturdy pair of hands guided her back onto the bed roll.

It was sometime later when she woke again. It was night now, and the palm fronds blocked out a swath of stars above her.

Thankfully her head was no longer swimming. She sat up gingerly to see Mick and Aterby sitting by a fire, their backs turned towards her. Aterby had a sizeable chunk of what looked like roasted meat in his hand, and her stomach rumbled. Embarrassingly, it was loud enough that the two men turned at the noise.

Mick shot her a grin, and Aterby inclined his head in an invitation to join them by the fire.

Before she'd even shuffled over to sit on a soft-looking patch of grass, Mick had risen and carved off a generous portion of meat from something cooking over the fire. He handed it to her on a thin metal plate with a smile.

"Thanks," she said, before devouring the meat in seconds.

"More?" he inquired with a smirk.

It was only then that she realised the man hadn't even sat back down yet.

"Yes please, if there's enough."

"Don't worry, there's plenty to go around," he returned, the smile falling off his face. He looked away for an instant before taking her plate and slicing off several more chunks with what appeared to be an extremely sharp knife.

She accepted the plate from him with another nod of thanks, and Mick went back to his place next to Aterby. She ate the second serve at a much more reasonable pace. It wasn't until she was well into the meal that she took the time to look around.

At first she thought Mick and Aterby had drawn the watch. As she scanned the area, she realised with a growing sense of dread that the two of them were the last men standing. Every pallet was occupied by a wounded man, and there weren't enough for every soldier.

She put the plate down, and the motion caused Aterby to look over and see her haunted expression reflected in the firelight.

"Millard made it too, and Erichs. Colbar's on that sleeping roll," he said, pointing at an injured man across the fire. "We've been taking turns bringing the wounded down from the other site. They should be back soon."

Johanna nodded. There were so few of them left. That Trelmaine wasn't one of them still left an empty pit in her stomach, but maybe she could do something for those who remained. She'd healed Mick's arm, and the man seemed fine. Better to check that though before she continued that line of thought.

"How's the arm?" She asked, half expecting him to say she'd done something wrong, or that he was still in pain.

"Perfect," he said, the grin returning.

When she'd first met him by the fire on the cliff, he'd been rude at best, even throwing a rock at her head. But when he smiled like that, it was like a mask falling away, or perhaps being put on. It was difficult to tell. The captain had trusted him. For now, that would have to be good enough.

"So no pain, no stiffness, or other weirdness?" she pressed.

"Weirdness?" he replied with a cocked eyebrow.

"You know what I mean," Johanna replied. "I barely remember how I performed that spell this morning and never should have tried it in such a disoriented state. I don't want to try it again unless I'm sure it worked correctly."

Mick considered her words, then rolled his shoulder as if suddenly unsure of his own body. He shrugged.

"Look, I won't even pretend to understand what you did, but if something went wrong, I can't tell what it was. I've already done three more trips up to the cliff to carry down stretchers. The arm is tired and strained, but no more so than the one that wasn't injured. Not sure what else I can say?"

Johanna looked at his honest expression and nodded. It seemed her fears were unfounded, after all.

"Ahhh, she's awake," a familiar voice said even as the sound of footsteps became audible a little up the path.

She couldn't help but smile when she saw Millard leading a stretcher carried at the other end by a man who must be Colbar. He was a heavy-set soldier with a bald head and black beard, which had grown out past military protocol.

The man nodded her way as he and Millard crossed the camp to place the latest stretcher in an empty spot across from where they were. He was conscious, but both his legs appeared broken.

This time, Aterby sliced off some of the meat and carried it over to him while Millard and Colbar got their own.

"How's the arm?" Millard asked as he found an empty piece of grass and sat.

Mick shrugged. "Armmy."

Millard chortled. "Good to hear."

Johanna looked down at her now empty plate with a nervous sigh. The spell had worked. Mick was fine.

Time to get on with this.

She stood, though not as gracefully as she would have liked, stumbling a step before regaining her legs. Her head was still not right, and the rest of her body had suffered days of abuse and deprivation, culminating in the beating she'd taken from that Imbic. It wouldn't stop her walking across the campsite and doing what she had to do. Many of the men on the pallets were in far worse shape than she. Those that had survived to this point, anyway.

She chose the man who'd just been brought into camp. He was already awake, and his injuries didn't seem too severe.

"Hello," he said when she knelt down next to him.

"Hi," Johanna replied. "You about ready to walk again, soldier?" she asked more confidently than she felt. If the man knew how much she doubted herself right now, he wouldn't even let her try.

"Yes, ma'am," the soldier replied, placing his plate beside him on the ground so she could work.

Joahnna nodded, then placed her hand over the break in his right leg. She had to concentrate, but the delving spell she had used earlier, and in her dreams, sprang into being with an almost audible click in her mind. It was becoming a reassuring sensation, letting her know she was actually *doing* something.

The strange sensation overcame her again as in her mind's eye she could suddenly feel what was happening inside the injured limb. The larger bone had snapped cleanly, and someone had done a passable job of re-orienting and immobilising the break so it would heal on its own in time. This one would be easy. She joined the bone together with the same connecting spell she'd used on Mick's flesh. By the time it was complete, even she couldn't tell where the two halves had been severed.

The man in front of her visibly relaxed, and she realised that with the bone now healed, his body was no longer sending out pain signals to his brain.

She repeated the process on his other leg, though this one was a bit trickier as the bone had splintered into several parts. It took her several minutes, and more than a little muttered cursing from the soldier as she manipulated the bone back to where the delving spell told her each segment was ready to be re-joined. Each time she completed a segment he would relax a little, then grimace again as she went on to the next piece. At some point, he just lay back and covered his face with his hands until she'd joined the last segments together. With a visible shudder, he sat up again and began undoing the splint knots on each leg before testing them gingerly with a slight bend. Even after everything she had just put him through, the man looked shocked when he attempted to put his weight on them, and they held.

"Worth it," he muttered as he gave her a toothy smile.

"Ready for duty," he said to Millard, throwing the sergeant a formal salute. "Orders?"

With only an instant of hesitation, Millard returned the gesture. He wasn't comfortable yet with being thrust into command.

"For now, eat and rest. At first light, we bring the rest of the wounded down from the camp. Speaking of which, Mick, Aterby, you're up. Mage Johanna, if you wouldn't mind going with them?"

Colbar gave him a sideways glance, but said nothing.

"Shouldn't I?" she said, motioning to the other injured men.

"Yes, but first I'd like you to heal as many of those at the other camp as you can. Every man you get moving on his own is less time and effort it will take to bring us all to a single defensible position again."

"Yes, of course," she agreed. The request made perfect sense, given that she'd need to heal all of them in the end. The order in which she did it was only relevant if one of them was succumbing to their injuries. The sad truth was, after days of deprivation and lack of anything but the most basic medical care, most of those who were going to pass into the black lady's embrace, already had.

As the sun peaked above the horizon, she glanced at Mick and Aterby, and with a small shrug the three of them headed back up the path towards the first camp. By now, the men there would be wondering where they were. Those who were conscious, or awake at this time of night. Leaving them had been terrible strategy, but what else could Millard have done? Two camps, four able men, and pairs needed to move each injured soldier.

Only one camp could be guarded. Leaving one man at either end would have meant the same pair of soldiers would have to carry all the injured themselves, an impossible task over that distance and terrain. Now that she was awake and functional, all that had changed. She could wait at the other end while the men ferried anyone too injured to be healed straight away. Hopefully, it wouldn't be needed. Hopefully, by morning, they would all be back together.

When calling for help, be careful whose attention you attract.
Excerpt from 'Advanced Warfare and Tactics.'

CHAPTER 12

THE BEACON

The night had passed without incident, and she had healed all but two of the soldiers at the original camp. Both had sustained bad head wounds that defied her ability to define and treat. Knitting ropy veins and fibrous muscles back together was one thing. Fixing a man's brain was entirely another.

There were nine of them now. Mick and Aterby, herself and the two unconscious men, and the four soldiers who were now back on their feet. Dawn had broken some time ago and there was just enough left in the supplies to make a thin porridge. Mick ordered the newly healed men to eat their fill, and once they were done, it was time to move on.

With the extra manpower, things were considerably easier, and both Mick and Aterby took an end to one of the unconscious men's stretchers while other soldiers took up the rear. The last pair packed what few supplies still existed and loaded them onto another stretcher.

Johanna found herself at a loose end and Aterby saw her looking around for a way to help.

"You've done your part," he said without preamble, glancing at her wounded arm. "It's a shame you magi can't heal yourselves. But save your strength, there's plenty more for you to do when we get back."

Johanna nodded. It seemed casting spells wasn't physically tiring, but the intense concentration required over the course of the night, on top of everything else, had left her with a thumping headache.

"Right then!" Mick said loudly enough to get the group's attention. "Off we go."

He led the way, with the freshly healed men in the middle, and Aterby's pair bringing up the rear. Johanna followed them after a last glance around the camp to make sure nothing important remained.

The morning sun crested the cliff behind her as they walked, and colourful birds flitted from tree to tree above. Up here, on this small part of the path, there was no sign of the destruction the massive wave had caused. That would not be the case a little closer to sea level.

It took longer to reach the new camp this time, the need to carry stretchers conspiring to make the trip seem far longer than it had the previous night. Even so, soon enough they descended to the site of the fight with the westerners, and to the current camp. From here she could see far enough to the west that the point where the trees petered out was clear. There was a short length of ground where most of the palms were snapped off at about waist height, and then nothing.

This might be the largest island in the chain, but even it had suffered catastrophic damage at its lower elevations. The sheltered northern beach where she had swum ashore was the only exception, and even that was now littered with washed up debris. She caught a waft of decay from fish stranded by the wave and left to rot in the sun. There just weren't enough predators on these islands to deal with them all.

She wondered again whether the lion had survived the second wave. She doubted it, but she'd probably never know, and she certainly wasn't going looking for it. Their two unexpected encounters had been more than enough.

Mick and Aterby led their stretchers over towards the fire, and with the help of the men on their other ends, placed them gently beside the other, still wounded soldiers. After adding the stretcher carrying the small pile of supplies to what they'd taken from the Nostahl, the newly recovered men found themselves a place in the shade to rest.

When she looked around, Millard was already watching her. He nodded in greeting and even gave her a small smile. She returned it without thinking. The captain might be gone, but she thought Millard would do a good job in her absence.

"That's it for the other site," Mick reported, once relieved of his burden.

Millard nodded, then seemed to realise that something more of a response was required now that he was in charge.

"Very good soldier, carry on," he said.

The words sounded uncomfortable even to her.

She didn't envy him the task of leading this fractured group of survivors.

There was a rustle in a bush behind her, and she jumped. Millard noticed too, and was on his feet in an instant.

"Back away," Aterby hissed as he rounded the large, dense foliage, a foot long knife in his hand which he clearly knew how to use.

"Come out now. If you have a weapon, don't bring it with you," Aterby called in a firm, commanding voice.

There was a moment of silence, then a frightened voice replied.

"Don't harm me, I'm not armed."

"Prove it," Aterby demanded.

"I'm coming out. Don't hurt me," the shaky voice repeated.

What emerged from the bushes was not at all what Johanna expected. The creature was bipedal, but covered in a matted, duck-egg blue coloured fur dotted with briars. It sported a long, lashing tail that reached almost to the ground, similar to that of a lemur, but its most striking feature was its eyes. They were huge. Double the size of a human's, maybe triple, with iris' the deep brown of a good honey. Its nose was tiny, but its face was expressive, and it was holding up its... hands? in an all too human gesture.

Arborii, some recessed portion of her mind supplied.

"Who are you?" the creature asked as it swayed, every word clear in perfect Jeranonian. "You're not part of the garrison."

"No," Millard answered as he walked towards the creature. "But you are."

Johanna stared at the creature... person, before her. In her shock at the arborii's appearance, she had completely missed noticing the tattered and filthy clothing it wore was an adapted version of the regular army uniform.

"Yes sir, Private Undu. Quartermaster for the garrison. Or at least I was..."

The arborii swayed again and sat heavily, gasping as he grasped at his back.

Johanna moved over to examine it and found the back of Undu's uniform soaked with blood.

"Lay down and let me heal this," she told him firmly.

For whatever reason, the arborii seemed on the verge of protesting, but then acceded, nearly collapsing as he lowered himself to the ground.

It was the work of a few minutes to slice away the uniform and dried blood which had matted into the arborii's fur. What she found wasn't promising. Unlike the clean cuts which had resulted from the enemy swords, this wound was more of a tear, jagged and messy.

"What did this?" she said, more to herself than the arborii.

"A tree branch," Undu replied anyway. "I was enjoying some free time in the forest canopy when the wave hit. Needless to say, it didn't go well. I've been trying to get back to the garrison ever since. I'm very glad to have run into you."

Johanna looked at Millard, whose eyebrows twitched up momentarily in surprise. "I'm sorry to be the one to tell you this, but there is no garrison. It's been entirely washed away."

The arborii pulled itself up on overly long forearms to look at the sergeant.

"What?"

"The wave," Millard said gently. "It destroyed everything on the islands below an elevation not much below this. As far as we can tell, there were no other survivors apart from the Nostahl we were hunting before the incident. We've now dealt with them as well."

The arborii's mouth moved, once, twice, then it lowered itself back to the ground with another grunt of pain.

"Thank you for telling me."

Joahnna's shoulders slumped. Undu might not be human, but his pain was obvious.

"I'm going to need some water and a brush to clean this wound," she said to Mick. "I'll need to get the fur out before I attempt to join the flesh back together."

Mick nodded, heading back to the supplies to get the things she would need.

"Can't you just use the Gift to clean it?" Undu asked in shock.

"I'm sorry, it's not that simple."

The arborii's face screwed up, and she couldn't tell if the expression was because she couldn't do it, or because of the pain that he now knew would come.

Mick was back soon enough, and she took custody of the supplies.

She lifted the bowl of water and poured some into the most matted section of the wound. Undu shivered and had to force himself not to pull away at its cool touch.

"Wait!" the arborii insisted before she could go any further. "If you're the ranger unit they ordered me to resupply last week, you aren't familiar with this island. You don't know that at the peak there is a signal fire kept ready for emergencies, bright enough to be seen from the mainland. Go there and light it. If the admiral defeated the western fleet, if Northwatch still stands, help will come."

"Thank you," Millard told him sincerely.

By now, much of the dried blood around the gash had softened, and Johanna called Aterby over. The man looked as though he knew how to use a knife. She explained the wound needed cleaning, and the fur removed before she could begin. Aterby looked daunted by the request, but after a glance at Millard went about the task without complaint. Undu passed out shortly after he started. It was better for everyone that way. Without interruption, they were able to complete the task, leaving the arborii's flesh whole, but missing a large strip of fur.

"Get a stretcher and put him somewhere more comfortable. He's one of ours now," Millard said to the unoccupied men.

*   *   *

Three hours later, she'd finished treating the rest of the wounded men in camp and her head was pounding, though her arm seemed slightly better. All she wanted was sleep. She moved back to her sleeping roll and closed her eyes. It helped a little.

Whatever else they may be, the Nostahl were proficient hunters. Mick was currently serving up portions of roast meat and a wedge of cheese for each of the men, all pilfered from the westerners' supplies.

Once they had cared for and changed the dressings of the wounded, she estimated they had two days' worth of water remaining if they rationed it. She may still have to do something about that. It could wait.

She didn't realise she'd drifted off until she felt a firm but gentle hand on her shoulder.

"You need to eat something," Millard said. "You're still not recovered fully yourself, and we have things to do."

Johanna sat up, her whole body stiff. How long had she been out? She checked the sun, dumbfounded to find it in a lower position than it had been a moment before, and in the wrong direction.

"I've been asleep since yesterday?" she said in alarm.

"Mm hmm," Mick said as he deposited a plateful of coconut, beef and even some cheese next to her. "Must have worked up quite the appetite by now."

Her stomach rumbled at the sight of the mismatched food. It was what they had. It was a feast compared to what she'd had since waking nine days ago on that other island, no memory and surrounded by dead bodies.

"Thanks Mick," she said, and the man gave her a grin before wandering off.

"When you're ready, we're going up to the peak to light that signal. We would have left yesterday, but Undu says there's a lock we won't get past without either you or the key, and since we don't have the key…"

She nodded as she gulped the water from the coconut, then scooped the flesh out with her fingers. Next, she attacked the wedge of cheese. It was dry and pungent with a strong, sharp taste which she found herself enjoying immensely.

"Right, I'll leave you to it," Millard said with a grin.

She nodded vaguely, far more interested in the roast meat, which she began devouring in alternate bites with the cheese. In less than two minutes, her plate was empty, and looking at it, Johanna wondered why she'd been so ravenous. It hadn't been that long since she'd eaten. In the end, she could only put it down to the same thing as her overly long slumber the day before. Her wounds were healing, and despite the abuse her body had suffered over the last week and more, she had access to regular food and water again. It seemed her body wanted to make full use of those resources while they lasted.

So be it.

She stood, leaving the plate where it was, and stretching. Her body ached all over, but at least some of that was from lying on the hard ground all night with only a sleeping roll beneath her. The fact she could tell the difference between that, and her other hurts, was encouraging. It meant the rest of her bumps, bruises, scrapes, and cuts were healing. She could move around well enough now that it didn't matter. Still, she was looking forward to the pain going away once and for all.

After walking off into the bush for a privy stop, she returned to Millard and told him she was ready to go. She wasn't entirely sure it was true, but like the sergeant had said, they had things to do. Water was still an issue, and until they got the signal burning, nobody was getting off this island.

"Alchemy is not for the fainthearted…"
Excerpt from a speech to new inductees by Grand Master Everyn of the Herbalists and Apothecaries Guild.

CHAPTER 13

THE BLAZE

There was only one peak on this island, and so it wasn't hard to head towards their destination. At least not intellectually.

The path was gruelling, with many spots so steep that Johanna had to use both her hands and feet to continue. At first, she had been hesitant about using the roots and spindly trees that jutted out of the soil as anchors, expecting them to pull out and leave her floundering at the slightest pressure. Now she was too tired to care. They had been walking for hours, her, Millard, and Undu, attempting to reach the emergency signal fire the arborii assured them waited at the peak.

This far up the island, the wave hadn't touched the land, and trees of every description stood witness to their passage. Birds were abundant, having taken shelter here when their previous homes had been obliterated, and their calls were thick in the air.

Unlike the rest of the days she had spent on the islands, today was overcast. A thick mass of clouds had moved in from the east earlier in the morning, and now everything was beginning to stick.

She looked up at the peak, at the jutting rock formation lying in wait behind the next copse of trees. The trail ahead was still intimidating, but no longer the distant summit it had appeared from down near the beach.

Millard called a break, and Johanna sat down on the grass without comment. Undu leapt gracefully onto a low tree branch and flattened himself onto it as if it were the most natural thing in the world.

Perhaps for his species it is.

There was so much she still didn't know, so many gaps. Or perhaps the holes in her memory were only about her own life, and she'd never actually known the rest. Why Undu appeared comfortable resting on his precarious branch, for instance. Was that something all arborii did, or just him? Until she was confident she had regained all of her memories, she would never know what it was she didn't know. What was missing and would eventually come back? What did she still have to learn for the very first time? Too much, she suspected.

They each took a drink from their canteens once they'd calmed their heart rate, and all too soon, Millard was calling for them to keep moving.

"Another half hour should see us there," Undu supplied at her long-suffering look.

She nodded briefly. She didn't have the energy for more.

Past hundred span high trees, and across boulders, and more of the pointed rock formations she had seen at her waking site than she could count, they made their way upward. Eventually, her foot caught on something.

She looked down in a mild daze and realised she was standing on the hard packed dirt of a well-maintained path. What was that doing there?

THE PATH OF PRIDE

"Good," Undu said as he reached the spot a moment later.

"There was a path up here all along?" Millard said in exasperation.

"Sure," Undu replied. "It leads to the garrison. This entire station exists to warn the mainland of an impending naval attack, so the path is maintained as a priority."

"Why didn't we just use it then?" Johanna asked, the words coming out a little more sharply than she'd intended.

Undu just stared at her. If he'd had eyelids, she suspected they would be blinking right now.

"The garrison is on the other side of the island, on the beach. It would have added a day to our trip. Once we've lit the beacon, we'll have as much time as we need. We can go back that way if you like?"

His head swivelled between the sergeant and mage, and Johanna had the abrupt realisation that the arborii was quite young, or at least inexperienced.

"This is your first assignment, isn't it, Undu?"

"Yes Mage," the arborii replied.

"You're doing fine," Millard assured him. "Let's get this done."

He motioned for the arborii to lead, and Undu nodded and continued up the path.

Millard grinned, and Johanna shook her head ruefully. Then again, in a way, it was hers as well.

They continued up the path for a short time, and Undu was good to his word.

Johanna rounded a jutting cliff edge which the path skirted and came in sight of a large double door recessed into the apex of the cliff. Four spans high, sealed tight, and composed of weather-rusted metal. It had to be the entrance to the beacon.

"Here we are," Undu said as he turned back towards them.

Millard raised his eyebrows as he examined the doors. "I don't suppose you have the key?"

Undu shook his head. "There were two. One for the garrison commander, and a spare. As quartermaster I knew where it was stored, but with the entire garrison washed away, I'm afraid that one is now at the bottom of the sea."

"Great," Millard replied. "Johanna, is there anything you can do about this?"

She had known it was coming, but that didn't make the fact they were once again relying on her unreliable skills any easier to swallow.

"I have no idea."

She walked the rest of the way to the enormous doors, twice as high as she herself was, and examined a raised area near the seam at the appropriate height. She lifted the flap of metal, and a small hole was revealed behind what must be a weatherproofing cover. It was just the right size to fit a large, sturdy key. Unfortunately, finding it didn't do them any good.

"Any other way in?" She asked.

"At the peak," Undu replied. "There's a hole in the roof with a staircase leading up to the mirror, but I don't know how to get there without going through this door."

She glanced back at Millard.

"Right," he said before heading around the cliff face to look for another way up.

As far as she could tell, the lock was a simple mechanical arrangement, but perhaps there was a better way to find out.

She closed her eyes and concentrated, hoping her idea would work.

It took her a few minutes, but she summoned up the delving spell she'd been using to assess the soldiers' wounds. As soon as she had it, she began probing the lock. Why couldn't she make other spells work like this? Perhaps it was just a matter of waiting for her memories to return. Certainly she could still cast spells, she just didn't know how most of them worked.

The lock was not complex, but the key it required was large and heavy. There was no chance she could use something thin to manipulate these heavy tumblers.

She let the spell drop. Hopefully Millard was having better luck.

An hour went by in relative silence while she sat in a nearby patch of shade, waited for Millard, and contemplated what else she could do. The frustrating thing was that she was sure that if she had her memories, this would be the simplest of tasks. All she had to do was move a few bits of metal and turn the lock. But how? The only two spells she could reliably cast were the delving spell, which, while useful, didn't allow her to manipulate the physical world. That and the joining spell she had used to heal the men's wounds. That would just fuse the lock into one piece, making it unusable.

"Well, that was a waste of time," Millard announced as he came back around the rock outcropping. "It's sheer cliff all the way around. How did you go?"

"Not much better."

"Undu. Any other ideas?" Millard asked as he approached the pair.

"Sorry sir. I've only been up here once during the

induction on my first day on the island. They didn't cover what to do if a massive wave swept away the entire garrison."

"Understood," Millard said.

The sergeant looked around in frustration. "We need to solve this."

"Can't you just use an earth spell and fashion a new key?" he asked. "I've seen plenty of magi manipulate physical objects. Surely you can take a rock or something and change its shape a little?"

Johanna stared at him for a moment. Was that something magi could do?

"Perhaps. If I knew how."

Millard sighed as he came and sat down next to them.

"Wouldn't it just be like everything else? Imagine, focus, initiate. That's what my grandfather used to say. The simplest thing in the world, but it only worked if you had the Gift."

"Your grandfather was a mage?" she asked, now more interested in his advice.

"An archmage. He died on the border during the invasion fourteen years ago."

"I'm sorry," Johanna replied. "What else did he say?"

Millard thought for a moment. "Well, he had this theory that the magi already had everything they needed to cast spells within them. He said that what most people thought of as learning magic was actually the individual learning to push aside their disbelief and accept what they already had within them."

Johanna frowned. "Then he believed that only our imagination holds us back, or lack thereof?"

"Exactly," Millard replied. "He used to say there was

nothing a properly focused mind could not achieve if the level of power matched that of the imagination. Except flying. He could never understand why he couldn't fly. It was the great frustration of his life that a lowly pigeon could do what even the most powerful archmage could not accomplish."

Undu laughed, but Johanna was deep in thought. She picked up a rock from nearby and stared at it, imagining it larger on one side, smaller in the middle, longer at one end. For long moments nothing happened, and her shoulders slumped, defeated. She had been sure they were on to something.

Millard was looking at her, realising what she was trying to do.

"One other thing he used to do during particularly arduous spell work, was to mutter, small steps, to himself. If that helps?"

Johanna thought about it for a long moment, then went back to her rock. She'd been trying to make it change in several ways at once. Maybe it wasn't that she couldn't do it, maybe she was having trouble imagining it? Once again she focused on the changes she was imagining, but only one. She visualised the small rock becoming thinner in the middle, and only that. There was a click in her mind, and the rock shifted in her grasp, thinning out in exactly the way she'd imagined.

"There you go!" Undu shouted, while Millard smiled.

For Johanna's part, she just stared, dumbfounded at the altered rock sitting in her hands. She'd acted out of pure reflex with the lion and when she'd killed the Imbic mutation. Her attempts at producing water had been erratic. Even healing the soldiers' wounds had been internal to their bodies and impossible to see. Having the rock change like that, exactly as she intended, and in full sight of them all was shocking. She didn't think she'd gained any fresh memories, but she'd meant to do that, and for the first time since waking on the other island, she smiled without reserve. Even if her memories never came back, she could relearn her skills, she could still be a mage!

A heady rush of confidence filled her, and she stood. She could do this. She walked back over to the lock hole and pushed the rock against it. But what shape did she need it to be? The delving spell would tell her.

It worked much faster this time, almost instantly in fact, and suddenly she could feel every texture, every contour inside the mechanism. She smiled again and concentrated on elongating the rock until it filled the inside of the lock. Next she pulled it out width wise until the delving spell told her she had contacted the tumblers. She pushed it a little further until there was a quiet click, and stopped. She nodded to herself and repeated the process for the four other tumblers. Once all of them were pushed back, she looked around with a slight grin to Millard and twisted the rock. There was a loud clunk and the left side of the large metal doors popped open a hand's width.

Undu jumped up, and Millard stood more sedately.

"Well done, Mage Joahnna," he said as the three of them took hold of the door and pulled it open the rest of the way.

It was stupid, but she couldn't help blushing slightly. She hid it well though by leaning into the door and pulling along with the others.

The three of them wrestled the door open, and Undu preceded them inside, the tip of his tail swaying in what she assumed was a good mood.

She looked around as they entered. The room was about ten spans wide at the base, built in a rounded, conical shape pointing towards the roof. Even the floor was something of a curved pit. More oddly, every surface, including the floor, was brass, polished and shined until she could see herself in it like a poor man's mirror. The centre of the room held wood for an enormous bonfire. A grainy white powder that looked a little like salt covered every part of it.

At the back of the room was a staircase leading up to a covered hole in the roof, and Undu headed straight for it.

"There's a few things we need to do before we can light it," he said, tail lashing slightly. "I may need your help again, Mage."

Millard shrugged when Johanna glanced at him, and together they followed the arborii up the circular metal staircase to the roof, while he opened the cover and preceded them outside. Like everything else in the room it was formed from a shining, burnished metal.

Johanna took the stairs quickly, there were only about twenty of them, and exited onto a ledge of the cliff they'd been trying to find their way onto before.

For a long moment she stopped, looking up at the huge circular mirror above her, hidden by the angle of the cliff until now. The apparatus was about five spans wide, concave, and angled to reflect light coming from the chamber below. She presumed it was aimed at a spot on the mainland where someone would see the beacon's light.

Millard was trying to exit the hatch behind her, and Johanna stopped staring long enough to get out of the sergeant's way.

"Over here," Undu called.

He was standing beside a cupboard sealed with a large lock, and Johanna picked up another small rock before he had to ask.

She moved over to the lock and pressed the rock against it. Imagining the rock changing, she repeated the process from before, and to her delight the lock sprang open when she turned her makeshift key.

It had worked again. The spell cooperated. Just like that, Johanna was sure she wouldn't have any more trouble controlling her powers. She just needed to remember what those powers were.

She took the lock of the cupboard and Undu swung the door open. Inside were a series of sealed clay pots with what appeared to be beeswax plugs which would melt in even the gentlest flame.

On each of the three shelves, a row of pots sat waiting. The top level pots each carried a label with the words 'enemy sighted' inscribed in neat font. The middle row was similar, but with 'enemy superior' inscribed on them instead, while the last row read, 'evacuation required'.

Glancing at Millard for confirmation, Undu reached in and took one of the latter pots. He then carried it over to a small bucket hooked up to a series of pulleys which disappeared inside a hole in the cliff.

"You can close that now, Mage," he said as he placed the pot inside the bucket.

Johanna did as he said, while Undu inspected the mirror. He seemed happy enough with what he found, then moved over to a crank set in the floor. Getting down on his knees, Undu strained against the metal handle for several seconds until it groaned and began to move. Once the mechanism was free, the handle seemed to turn readily enough. A section of metal plating began rotating away from what she assumed must be the opening at the aperture of the room below. It took a few minutes, and Millard spelled the puffing Undu before the task was complete, but there were no further complications.

"Almost done," Undu told them once Millard locked the crank into its final resting place. "Time to go."

He motioned for them to head back down the stairs, and the three of them left the sheltered ledge. Undu went last and closed the hatch behind him, rendering the room one seamless reflecting cone. Only the hole in the roof, which the crank had opened, now exposed the room to the outside world.

"So how do we light it?" Millard asked as Undu headed for the door.

"We don't. The Alchemists Guild provides the elements used to make the beacon. If you were to look at them once burning, they would blind you instantly. Or at least that's what the captain told us when he brought us up here."

"That's what's in the bucket? Some kind of catalyst?"

"Sorry Mage Johanna, I'm not familiar with that term. All I was told is that once we close the doors, the pot will drop, and the beacon will light."

"Good enough," Millard assured him.

Undu nodded, and they exited through the same double doors they'd used to enter. Millard pushed one side closed and Undu took the other, and together they sealed the doors tight, completing the inner symmetry of the reflecting room.

There was a deep rumble from inside, and a moment later they were all forced to cover their eyes as a blinding, deep red shaft of light appeared in the sky just above them.

The beam hit the mirror, reflecting off it at right angles and heading south to the mainland in a visible line.

"Whoa," Millard said once their eyes had adjusted to the unnatural glare. Undu just grinned at the beam of light emanating from the chamber, reflecting off the mirror, and holding steady to the horizon, even in broad daylight.

They inspected their handiwork and Johanna gave the others a smile.

"Yeah," she said. "That should probably do it…"

Desiring something does not mean the world will grant it to you.
Terraliv saying.

CHAPTER 14

KINGFISHER

It had taken the rest of the afternoon, an uncomfortable night on the trail, and some of the next morning to return to their temporary camp. When they did, Johanna was grateful to find Mick waiting for them with rations of cooked meat and potatoes the men must have found somewhere from the night before. At least she presumed it wasn't their breakfast, with Mick in charge of the supplies though, who knew?

Aterby and Colbar had welcomed her back, and most of the others seemed happy to see her and Millard. Undu they were a little less warm to, but then the arborii had not yet had the chance to bond with them as she had.

Helping to light the beacon would no doubt help him break down that barrier.

The three of them ate their meals in silence. There was little need to report since the line of deep red light had continued into the night before fading away about an hour after dark. They had all seen it.

Once they had eaten, and rested for a bit, Millard stood to address the remaining men.

"All right, you all saw the signal last night. A ship will come for us. We'll need to be ready when it gets here.

Therefore, today's task is moving the camp down to the beach, or what's left of it, near where the docks used to stand. They may not be there anymore, but the water should still be deep enough for a ship to get in close and send out their lifeboats to come get us."

There were nods and smiles all around, and even a few cheers.

Millard grinned. "Don't get too excited just yet, there's plenty of work still to do. We don't know how long it will take the rescue ship to arrive, so we need to take everything with us. The good news is that with Mage Johanna able to heal most of you, Mick, Aterby, Colbar and I won't have to haul your sorry backsides around the island anymore. The bad news is, now you have to walk for yourselves. No more lying about watching the palm fronds wave."

There were a few guffaws, and Millard looked around at them all before nodding, satisfied at whatever he saw.

"It's done. The cost was steep on this one, I'm not going to lie. But we survived everything this mission has thrown against us, and achieved every objective. Captain Trelmaine would be proud that we held the line despite everything we've endured."

He stopped for a minute, glanced at the ground, and continued.

"And what would the captain order us to do after every victory?"

"Let's pick up our gear and go home!" Mick shouted in a fair approximation of Trelmaine's voice.

"Indeed," Millard said. "Let's do just that."

This time there were no cheers, but a few of the men saluted. Moments later they were moving off to see that the gear, and two remaining injured men, were moved safely down to the beach.

*   *   *

It was two days later when Aterby spotted sails on the horizon.

The trip down to the beach had been arduous, but not otherwise challenging, and the new camp was set up well before sundown. Where the garrison fort had stood, was now only blank stone bedrock with a few rough patches where the deepest level of foundations had held against the initial wave.

This part of the island faced west, but there was nothing protecting it from the south. Johanna remembered the wave obliterating the first small island, knocking enough mass off the top that it no longer stood above the waves. The fort would have been smashed like kindling under that kind of pressure. At sea level, the docks may as well never have existed for all the evidence they left behind. Millard had to order a bonfire built and kept alight just so the rescue ship would know where on the island to approach.

Aterby yelled down the news from his vantage point on a cliff above camp, and the bonfire had been lit. A little less than three hours later, the ship had dropped anchor, and a lifeboat was heading towards them.

Johanna watched it anxiously, willing the small vessel across the choppy surf. There were four sailors rowing, and what appeared to be an officer sitting at the rear. The boat could hold perhaps ten more occupants. They would have to make a few trips.

As the boat ran up onto the smooth rock of what had

once been a beach, the two sailors at the front leapt out and began beaching the craft. Several of her own men ran over to help them pull it up onto land so it wouldn't slide back out to sea. The other sailors jumped ship to help once they were in shallow enough water, and the officer strode to the front with practised ease and leapt straight onto dry ground.

"Who's in charge here?" he demanded, looking around at the weary, ragtag group of rangers and soldiers before spotting her blue-lined mage's cloak.

"Excuse my manner, Mage, but what happened here? Where is the garrison? The docks? The men?"

Johanna didn't answer him right away. She should have been expecting this, but with Millard doing a fine job of commanding the remaining men, she had been more than happy to let him take charge of the situation. But that luxury was over now she supposed. In the real world, Sergeants didn't give orders to magi.

Millard saw her hesitation and nodded minutely to indicate that this was how things were supposed to work.

She swallowed, suddenly nervous.

"Your name?" she asked instead, buying a little more time.

"Commander Wrigley, X.O. of the Kingfisher," the man supplied.

Johanna looked him up and down. His black hair was short, his face clean-shaven, and his body well-muscled in all the right places. He was also very obviously the kind of man who knew how good he looked and took a little too much pride in it. That he'd allowed his men to pull the boat from the surf while he himself jumped onto dry ground completed her impression of him.

"All you need to know for now is that there was a natural disaster, and that this is all the survivors on the island. Please start ferrying us over to your ship."

That sounded official enough.

Wrigley coughed in a clearly practised affectation.

"I can't do that, Mage..."

"Johanna," she replied.

"Mage Johanna, to do what you ask would mean abandoning the entirety of the Bulwark Islands if the western fleet prevails. I don't have the authority to give such an order."

For a long moment Johanna just stared at the man in disbelief.

"You don't have the authority to rescue us, after being sent to rescue us..? Take me to your captain, we're done here. Millard, you're with me. The rest of you men stay put, we'll get this nonsense sorted and we'll be on our way soon."

The soldiers were not happy, but no one went so far as to publicly object.

"Launch the boat," she ordered Wrigley, barely looking at the man as Millard helped her on board.

The man had the temerity to roll his eyes at his sailors, but they obeyed her just the same. Millard pushed with the others and as the lifeboat took float, they all scrambled back into the craft and took up oars to return to the ship.

The voyage wasn't long. The water of the cove was deep to accommodate the docks which had stood there for centuries, until last week. As a result, the Kingfisher was anchored relatively close in. Someone dropped a rope ladder over the side as they approached, and two of the sailors tied the boat to the ship while Wrigley motioned for her to ascend first. Not wanting to appear hesitant, she agreed, then noticed Millard step bodily in the way of the ladder as the commander attempted to follow her up. Millard crossed his arms and glared at the man, who was studiously pretending not to care which order they returned to the ship.

A hand reached out as she approached the deck, and she took the offer whilst she clambered over the rail. A moment later Millard appeared, followed by Wrigley, at which point she turned her attention to the man waiting on the forecastle.

The captain was deep in conversation with one of his officers and appeared not to be expecting them. When he noticed her approaching, he raised an eyebrow and turned to face her.

"Welcome to the Kingfisher, Mage. I'm Captain Henely," he said politely. "Please excuse my ignorance, but I wasn't aware there were any magi assigned here."

"It's a long story captain, suffice it to say I was not part of the garrison. I have sixteen more survivors on the island in need of evacuation, two of whom are unconscious."

Henely just looked out at where the garrison fort should have been and asked the obvious question. "First things first. What happened here?"

Johanna just sighed. Did she really have to go through this again? "There was a tsunami. One the size and power of which I have never even heard. It scoured the islands of everything below a certain elevation not protected on the lea side of the bigger islands. The garrison never stood a chance. The only reason we survived was that my men were patrolling for western survivors near the peak as part for their detached ranger duties. I was on the island to the west on other business. We've cleared the island of any further western presence, but lost several soldiers, including the commander of the unit to an Imbic mutation and band of Nostahl. We have no supplies to speak of, no shelter, no fresh water other than what I can pull from the air. We need you to take us home."

The captain's brow had drawn steadily down as she made the report. "Were there no survivors from the garrison at all?"

"An arborii quartermaster named Undu. He's with my men."

"I see," Henely said, deflating. "Wrigley, you have the helm."

Without another word, the captain left the forecastle, crossed the deck, and entered his private cabin. Johanna felt her mouth go slack. Millard watched him go in disbelief.

"What kind of messed up ship are you people running here?"

Wrigley seemed to come back to the present, his gaze turning hard as he looked away from where Henely had disappeared.

"Captain Henely's brother was stationed here. You'll excuse him if he takes a private moment to grieve his loss, Sergeant."

Millard had the good grace to look away and even blush slightly.

"I apologise, Commander," he said eventually. "It's been a very long week."

"For us all," Wrigley responded.

Johanna frowned slightly, thinking the words just more

of the man's bravado, but then she noticed the scoring along the ship's rails. They appeared to have sustained damage at multiple points from sword or axe blows. What's more, she noticed evidence that part of the deck had been on fire to the aft of the ship, and the main mast had suffered a similar type of damage to the rails.

"You've been in battle recently?" she asked.

Wrigley nodded.

"Two days ago. The fleet was still in combat with the western flotilla as they attempted to reach the mainland. When Admiral Harol ordered us to break off from the pursuit and come to your aid, we were already engaged with an Augrahl ship. We expected a flood of Nostahl when they pulled in beside us, but it was filled with actual Augrahl warriors. We saved the ship, but it cost us a third of the crew to repulse their boarding party. The Marigold managed a broadside into the enemy ships' flank before they could try again. We were barely able to cut the grappling ropes before it sank and took us down with it."

"I'm sorry," Johanna told him.

"Which is why we can't just abandon the Bulwark Islands. If any of the western fleet survives to retreat this far, they could go to ground here. It could take years for us to root them all out."

Johanna just stared at him. She knew it was true. She also knew they couldn't survive what he seemed to be implying.

"We can't stay here Commander," Millard repeated. "Even if what you're saying is true, and does in fact happen, the first shipload of troops that makes landfall will sweep us away at their leisure."

"You have a duty…" Wrigley responded.

"Not this one," Johanna interrupted.

"Only one of the survivors is even stationed here. Do you propose to leave him on his own? Or for the rest of these men, and myself, to abandon our own duties on the mainland?"

"I propose that you all stay here and do your duty as part of the king's greater military. We'll leave you what supplies we can afford and then get back to the fight. Once we've defeated the westerners, we'll come back with a proper relief convoy to rebuild the garrison."

Johanna felt her mouth open and close dumbly.

"That would take phases," Millard said. "And relies on you actually winning the battle and surviving to report what happened here. Otherwise you're just abandoning us to our deaths."

"You wouldn't be the first," Wrigley said, his eyes becoming unfocused for an instant as some memory pushed its way to the surface. "At the point we received orders to come investigate the signal, we'd already lost over sixty ships. By the time we get back…"

A figure appeared at the ladder to the forecastle and Captain Henley re-joined them, his face and manner now composed. It was a thin veneer.

"Commander, why is the boat not in the water? We have soldiers to evacuate."

"But, Captain," Wrigley protested.

"That's an order, Commander."

Wrigley's shoulders slumped, but he left without another word to carry out the captain's will.

"Please excuse my X.O. He's very good at killing our enemies, but not so great at diplomacy with friends."

"I'm sorry for your loss," Johanna said. "The disaster

here was of monumental proportions, for what it's worth, I doubt your brother suffered."

Henely nodded slowly.

"Thank you, Mage…" He faltered.

"Johanna," she said, introducing herself. "This is sergeant Millard of the ranger corps, he's in command of the remaining men."

"Pleased to meet you both. As soon as the rest of the survivors are on board, we'll weigh anchor and head south."

"Thank you," Johanna said in relief. "Commander Wrigley didn't seem inclined to take us at all."

"And under normal circumstances I'd see his point. But we're in the middle of an invasion, and the fight's there, not here. We've already lost a significant portion of our crew, and I expect you and your men to fight alongside ours when the time comes. That's the price of your passage."

Johanna found she'd run out of arguments. She didn't remember everything, far from it. But she expected that as a mage there would be some kind of law requiring her to defend Jeranon from its enemies when the need arose. Millard saluted as if the request were an honour, and the captain nodded, taking it for done.

"Gambult!" Henely bellowed, and a moment later a boy, no more than sixteen, poked his head up the ladder.

"Show Mage Johanna to Lieutenant Saxon's old room. Sergeant Millard, your men will have to bunk with my sailors below decks."

He sighed before adding, "There will be sufficient space for you all."

"Aye sir," Millard answered respectfully.

"Please follow me," Gambult said once it was clear their conversation was over.

"Thank you, Captain," Johanna said again as she passed him.

Once she was down off the ladder the captain sighed and said under his breath.

"Don't thank me yet, you haven't seen what's coming

A thing exists in our minds. Whether the physical world reflects our intent depends only on how well we shape reality to our will.
Excerpt from 'The Gift'.

CHAPTER 15

THE NOTION OF REFUGE

Two days had passed since they'd left the Bulwark Islands and all its destruction behind. They were heading south, and they'd been able to see the glow and smudge of smoke on the horizon since this morning.

The crew of the Kingfisher was going about their work, though very little conversation was apparent this day. Both soldiers and sailors were too focused on what was about to happen to care about making small talk.

"How long?" Johanna asked Captain Henely as she came to stand beside him at the prow of the ship. Her arm was still bandaged, but she had done away with the sling. It seemed apparent now that the bone had not been broken, just severely jarred by the Imbic mutation.

"After nightfall," he responded. "Unless we encounter resistance further out."

Johanna's hands tightened on the rail. If the western invasion fleet could spare ships from the battle to hunt for outliers like them, the king's forces had already lost.

"That smoke plume is coming from the area around Northwatch. We'll join the fleet there and bolster their forces with whatever we can muster. With any luck, the westerners will see it as a primary target and attack. If they do, we can catch them between the fleet and the castle."

Johanna frowned. "You want them to attack Northwatch?" she asked. "Can the castle repel that many invaders?"

The captain shrugged. "Doubtful, but there are only two real options for their fleet at this point. Either they concentrate their forces on a fortified position, doing as much damage to our military infrastructure as possible, or they make landfall at a random location. If they abandon the ships and scatter into the hills in small groups, they could depopulate a significant portion of the region before the army can locate and eliminate them all. If they choose that approach it will be largely out of our hands."

Johanna winced. The memory of the fight with the Nostahl and a single Imbic mutation all too fresh. She'd barely survived the encounter herself. The civilians in the area would have no chance at all.

"You're not a battlemage, are you?"

Johanna looked at the captain for a long moment, deciding how much to share.

"No," she said at length. "I can do some damage, but it's not my area of expertise."

Henely nodded slowly. "Might be time to branch out."

There wasn't anything more to say, and as the captain walked away to go about his business, she stayed at the prow.

There was nothing to see from this far out of course. The sailor up in the crow's nest would let them know when he sighted an enemy sail.

An hour ago they'd passed a stretch of debris. Scorched rope and splintered wood which hadn't quite sunk yet were accompanied by a half dozen Nostahl clinging to the tangle like a raft. No one even batted an eye when the X.O. ordered the archers to finish them.

The ship hadn't slowed, and Johanna became uncomfortably aware of just how little a single life meant in a battle on this scale. She had no illusions that had it been the other way around, the Nostahl would have done any different.

The day wore on. Each minute felt like an hour, every hour an age. There was nothing for her to do except wait for a battle she was ill equipped to endure. They would fight bravely, this mixed crew, she suspected. In the end though they would expect her to back them up, to be their failsafe in case all else failed. She would do her best, but inwardly she was prepared to admit she hoped that smoke smudge on the horizon was the king's fleet already having sunk the western invaders. If the battle was already over, she could report in to whichever archmage was present, and then finally be on her way home.

Two hours after midday, the lookout cried 'ships hoy!'

In instants, Henely was beside her at the prow, spyglass out and extended before she even knew he was there.

"Looks like two ships," he said after studying the sea before them. "Too far out to tell, but they seem to be grappled."

"X.O.," he called in a loud but calm voice.

"Aye sir, what's the order?" Wrigley called back from the main deck.

"Battle stations," Henely replied, setting off a flurry of orders from Wrigley to the crew.

Men went running in every direction, each knowing where to go and what to do. Despite Wrigley's unwelcoming manner when they'd come on board, this was a good ship, she realised.

A few minutes later her men were climbing on board, still dressed in armour heavier than usual for a ship's crew. Millard came up the ladder to join them, and seeing the fight still a way off, visibly relaxed.

"My men have experience with boarding actions, so we'll take the offensive role," Henely said as he turned to them. "Your unit will remain on this ship as defence since your armour is better suited to a sustained fight. Tell your men to stay away from the rails if fighting breaks out. If they go overboard wearing that gear, they'll drown before they can get it off and swim back to the surface."

"Sir," Millard responded, and left again to pass the word to his fourteen remaining men. That was if you included Undu in the count.

Millard gave her a reassuring grin as he disappeared back down the ladder, but by the time she looked back, Henely was already looking ahead through the spyglass again. He lowered it with a frown.

"I don't like this," he said, handing her the long metal tube with its inserts of ground glass. "I see one of ours and one of theirs grappled together, and plenty of bodies on the deck of either ship, but no fighting."

"Maybe we already won?" she offered. Even as she heard the words out loud, she knew they didn't sound right.

"No. If our crew had won, they would have separated and returned to the fight. I would have expected the same of the western crew, but perhaps they're laying low, waiting to ambush a rescue ship? Either way, since that's an obvious ploy, this doesn't make much sense."

Johanna nodded as she passed the spyglass back.

A long hour passed as they closed with the derelict pair of ships. Where were their crews?

When they were close enough to see the Jeranonian ship's name on the hull with their own eyes, and still there was no movement, the captain scowled.

"X.O., bring us alongside the 'Tall Oaks' and board with prejudice. Secure the ship, then move on to the enemy vessel."

"Moving to intercept, Sir," Wrigley called back, before issuing the specific orders to the crew.

In what felt like no time at all after the anticipation of the last two days, The Kingfisher slid in beside the Tall Oaks and coasted to a halt. Sailors threw thick, metal tipped grappling lines across the gap and secured the ships together with a gentle bump.

Every sailor not needed for the docking manoeuvre was waiting on deck, weapons out and ready for the order to board.

"Now!" Wrigley yelled, and as one they surged forward in a well-practised formation that let them leap the small gap between ships without getting in each other's way. Once they were all across, there was a moment of hesitation, but the expected swarm of enemy ambushers never materialised.

"Right, alpha shift head aft, beta shift with me."

She could hear Wrigley from across the other deck, and Henely had been right, the man was in his element here. The sailors disappeared into the belly of the ship, some fore and some aft. For long moments, all Johanna could do was strain to hear the ring of metal on metal that would signify the crew had been met with violence below decks. But there was nothing. Or was it just that she couldn't hear it from here?

A minute passed, two, then three. Henely shifted his weight in a silent gesture of unease beside her. What was happening down there? Why was this taking so…

The aft hatch opened, and Wrigley came striding out. His hand was on his weapon, but the blade remained sheathed.

"No survivors, Sir, but there's evidence they won the fight. A good portion of the crew are lined up below decks in a respectful manner, not something the westerners would do."

Henely's scowl deepened. "Very well, board and secure the enemy ship," he called back.

It took another minute for the boarding party to gather on deck, then Wrigley gave the order. They dashed up the thin walkways the enemy ship had used to board them, crossing over to the rival deck. Again there was a pause, again no one rushed out from below decks to greet them with bared blades, and Wrigley ordered his men to go below.

The sun shone down on Johanna as they waited, the pleasant breeze seeming at odds with how she felt she should be feeling. Henely and his men could be dying right now as they searched the western ship, and yet the day was rather pleasant. Or they could be fine. But really, what were the chances of both vessels being abandoned?

The wait this time was longer. Four minutes, then five passed. She looked down at the main deck and Millard shook his head. It had been too long.

Henely took a deep breath, but before he could give his next order Wrigley came back on deck. The captain let the breath go with a sigh of relief and Wrigley returned to the Tall Oaks so he could report.

"Three survivors, sir. All crew of the Tall Oaks. I'm transferring them across now. Other than that, all positions are secure."

Wrigley returned to the enemy boat to coordinate his men. A short while later some of their sailors helped the three survivors, all of whom showed the scars of battle, onto the deck of the Kingfisher.

Johanna motioned to the men, and the captain nodded his approval. It was a moment's journey to descend the ladder from forecastle to main deck, and as soon as the sailors saw her they began smiling.

"See boys, told you we'd make it," a man with an officer's uniform said with cheer.

Johanna ignored him as his wounds seemed confined to a large bruise on his head. The man to his right had two stab wounds in his left arm though, so she got to work on him first. She repeated the process she'd used on her own men during their time on the island. Despite the delicate work, this set of spells, at least, seemed well in her control. It was comforting to know that with practice, if nothing else, she could regain her skills. For good measure she used the delving spell again, this time across the man's whole body, but found no other wounds.

"Thank you, Mage," the man said with a grin, stretching the now healthy flesh as if to test out her work.

"You're welcome," she replied, but her attention was already on the final sailor.

The man was limping, and after running the delving spell over him discovered he had a cracked pelvis. She made the others help him to the floor, and once he was laying down healed the offending bone. It wasn't until she'd finished healing the man that it occurred to her that she'd done it without having to see the injury with her own eyes. She'd relied entirely on the delving. For a moment she wondered if she'd made a mistake, but then the man stood, jumped up and down a few times, and laughed.

"Very pleased to be meetin' you, Mage," he said in a reverberatingly deep voice. "I no' be feelin' this spry since I be twenty years old," he boomed with a thick Sunset Isles accent.

"You're welcome," Johanna told him with a grin. There was something open and honest about the large man that made her want to trust him.

For good measure she ran the delving spell over him, and then the officer once more, but neither of them was carrying any further wounds that required her attention.

By the time she was done, the captain had joined them on the main deck with a thoughtful look on his face.

The officer saluted as Henely approached, and the captain returned the gesture.

"Report," was the only greeting he gave though.

"Yes, Sir. We were engaged by western forces just after sunrise yesterday. After a three hour chase they caught us and boarded with a mixture of Augrahl, Nostahl, and one Imbic shock troop. Vicious brute that one, had to set it on fire to clear it from the deck. When their first wave failed, they just kept sending more troops, grinding us down until we were sure we were dead. It wasn't until Hartley here killed their captain that we realised what they'd done," he said, motioning to the Sunset Islander. "I've seen nothing like it, Sir. They just kept coming. I can only assume their captain was so enraged by our continued resistance that he continued sending more and more troops until he realised he'd over-committed and couldn't sail home. Then thrown the rest at us out of spite. When they ran out of bodies, we waited a full day before sneaking on to their ship only to find it empty. It was, creepy, Sir. The quiet of it. We kept expecting there to be more. Then you came to our rescue."

Henely nodded. "That's quite the tale. Status of the ships?"

"Good, Sir," the officer replied. "We took a glancing blow when they attempted to ram us, but our helmsman, Maker rest his soul, avoided the worst of it. The rest was a boarding action which resulted in little structural damage to either vessel. If I didn't know better, I'd swear their aim was to capture, not destroy us."

Henely nodded again, considering the man's words. After a long moment he called over the ship's railing.

"X.O."

Wrigley appeared on the western ships' deck a moment later.

"Rig that ship for towing by the Tall Oaks!"

Wrigley gave a salute rather than shout back, and the officer in front of them raised his eyebrows.

"With all due respect, Captain, I can't run the Tall Oaks with just the three of us."

"Of course not, that's why I'm going to put fifteen of my sailors under your command while you tow the western warship east and then south to Nestarn. That should be far enough to avoid the fighting."

"Me, Sir? I was fourth in command. I have extremely limited experience as captain," he said discretely.

"You can sail?" Henely asked directly.

"Aye Sir, I can sail," the man replied.

"Good, you won't have enough crew to fight, so stay well clear, and if you see sails on the horizon, run."

"Sir, why Nestarn. It's not a major military port?"

"Simple, I don't know how this battle is going, but win, lose, or draw, at the time we were called away, the fleet had already lost half its ships. Jeranon will need to replace those losses. We don't have enough crew to effectively fight these ships right now, so we're going to preserve them for later. Sail for Nestarn, and send word to Miralthrall that the situation here is not under control. They'll need to reinforce the northern coast from Harverness to Nestarn for some time to make sure the westerners didn't scatter troops all over the region."

The officer gave a smart salute. "We'll get it done, Sir."

"Yes you will."

Henely cleared his throat before continuing in a voice modulated for all those around to hear.

"I hereby grant you a field promotion to the rank of commander, along with all the titles and responsibilities that come with both that rank, and interim command of the Tall Oaks. Return to your ship, Commander. Carry out your mission."

The officer gave him a crisp salute while the big sailor clapped him on the back, and just like that the three men were gone.

"X.O."

Wrigley appeared as if by magic, and Henely didn't miss a beat.

"Gamma shift is to collect any personal items they have on board and report to the Tall Oaks for reassignment."

For a long moment Wrigley's jaw worked, making no sound. The man was not happy.

"Sir, might we have a word in private," he asked about as politely as a dog straining against a lead.

"Certainly. Come to my cabin after you've carried out my orders and we'll discuss whatever's on your mind," Henely replied.

Wrigley's lips compressed to the point of whiteness, and he turned on his heel and stalked away.

"That's going to be a fun conversation," he muttered.

Johanna didn't think the comment was meant for her ears, but responded anyway.

"Is that something you need help with?" she asked just as quietly.

Henely seemed surprised that she'd heard him, but shook his head.

"He thinks I'm reducing our ability to fight the enemy. He's right. He's also not looking at a big enough picture. If we lose this fight, those might be the only two military ships Jeranon has to stand watch in the north in days to come. They won't be able to stop an invasion, but properly positioned they will give us enough warning to put countermeasures in place."

"Do you think that's likely, that we'll lose this fight?"

Henely shrugged. "We'll be under way soon. We'll know more once the sun goes down."

Consequence is not a straight line, but rather, a ripple.
Arborii Proverb.

CHAPTER 16

RIPPLES

They'd lost time with their rescue of the Tall Oaks and its remaining crew, and an hour after sundown they were still not in sight of land. From the flashes on the horizon, the battle still raged in the sea near Northwatch. But were those the two navies still fighting, or was the western fleet already assaulting the castle?

"Ten degrees to port," Henely ordered the helmsman. "I want to come to Northwatch from a westerly bearing."

"Aye, Captain, ten degrees to port," the sailor confirmed, turning the wheel slightly as he spoke.

There was nothing to do but wait while the crew went about their tasks. Johanna found she hated waiting, and she wasn't alone. Everybody knew they were likely in for a fight during the next few hours and nobody could sleep. As a result, the deck was full of sailors and soldiers milling about and in the way. It had reached the point where Wrigley had ordered some of them back below deck. Millard stood with them up here on the quarterdeck, and Johanna could see Aterby and Mick talking as they leant against the port rail down near the mainmast. Each of them had escaped the X.O.'s cull.

The sea on which they coasted was calm tonight, though

a crisp wind blew them towards their destination, and visibility was good due to a full moon above.

Another hour passed, and then another, and despite the tenseness of the situation, Johanna found herself getting sleepy as the Kingfisher rose and dipped on the back of each gentle wave. Maybe there was still time to go below decks and get a few minutes or an hour of sleep?

"Land Ho!" a sailor cried from the crow's nest, bringing her back to the present with a jolt. To the east, the flashes and glow of battle continued, but here on this part of the coast, all was quiet.

"Helmsman, follow the coast east at a distance of one mile."

Henely turned to her then. "Hopefully this way we'll enter the battle on the side our own ships are positioned on."

"What if the fleets are oriented differently than you expect?" Johanna asked without thinking.

Henely gave her a sideways look and a wry grin. "Remember that talk we had about branching out?"

Johanna swallowed nervously. "I'll do my best."

Henely lifted his spyglass, though what he could see in this dim light was anybody's guess.

To the south, sheer rock cliffs fifty spans high dominated the coastline, diving straight into deep water. Even this far from shore, the Kingfisher would be closer to the land than the seabed as the crow flew. The thought made her a little nervous. Who really knew what was down there, after all?

The repetitive sound on the deck next to her became annoying as her mind consciously registered the tapping of the captain's foot. He seemed nervous.

"What is it?" she asked.

"I don't know. Something... We should be able to see Northwatch once we clear the next cliff outcropping."

The conversation stuttered to a halt as Henely went back to surveying the coast with his spyglass. The tapping started again.

She strained to see some detail in the darkness, but from this far out, the jagged cliffs hid everything but the first line of trees at their peak.

"What's all that down near the cliffs?" She asked, a sinking feeling making its way through her gut.

Henely refocused his attention on sea level and frowned without taking the spyglass from his eye.

"Looks like debris, from the battle maybe? There's a lot, whatever it is."

The helmsman corrected course to take them around the final large outcropping and Johanna realised what she was seeing.

"It's not from the battle. This is what the islands looked like the morning after the wave hit."

Henely stared at her for a long moment, her words so dire that for an instant he couldn't comprehend their meaning. He shook his head in denial and hurried to lift the spyglass again as they began rounding the cliff.

Even in this dim light, she could pinpoint the moment he saw it. The captain's mouth sagged down, and for a few seconds he forgot even to breathe. The spyglass dropped to his side as he struggled to speak.

"It's gone..." he whispered. "The entire castle. It's just gone."

Johanna nodded sadly. If the wave had hit here as hard as it had in the islands, even the stone castle's mortar would not have held at sea level. Like there, the shallow, rocky beach where the cliffs broke, and Northwatch had been situated, was scoured to bedrock. Only a massive tangle of debris remained, blocking the entire incline. They couldn't have made landfall there if they'd wanted. To either side of the incline, cliffs loomed, and as the Kingfisher continued east, the watchtower on the western cliff was revealed. The wave must not have breached the cliffs here, at least not with enough force to topple the stone tower. Even the trees visible at the edge of the cliff seemed untouched. It took her a moment to realise the shallow gap in the cliffs where Northwatch and its docks had been located must have acted like a funnel. The one sloped area amongst the cliffs would have amplified the force of the wave as it sought to push up from the ocean floor. They'd never had a chance. Meanwhile, the fleet had coasted along the top of the sea, oblivious to the apocalyptic destruction approaching as it thundered toward them along the seabed below.

The Kingfisher coasted past the tower, which might be armed to the teeth, or deserted. In this dark, there was no way to tell. What they could see was the flash and glow now visible on the horizon. The low grumbles that reached them even at this distance could almost have been thunder, but she suspected they were something far more sinister.

"I hope your people are ready for this," Henely said a few moments later.

She nodded that they were, but suspected he was asking about her in particular. He knew she was no battlemage, but she hadn't seen fit to tell him about the giant holes in her memory.

Holes. It was a kind description. Her brain felt like a spiderweb which a bird had flown through and damaged beyond repair. Some strands remained strong and in place, the rest was just gone.

Halfway to the horizon, a fire started. From here, it was impossible to tell if it was one of theirs or a western ship. Whatever it was, the blaze spread quickly and didn't let up until the vessel submerged beneath the waves.

"Light and noise discipline! Prepare the cannons! Prepare to repel boarders!" Henely called. All around the ship, lanterns were doused as the Kingfisher prepared to approach the tangle of ships still engaged in what looked to have disintegrated into a free-for-all.

Dozens of ships were now visible as silhouettes, lit up as a cannon flashed, or another source of light appeared. A handful of spells were being cast, but in all, the Gift was only a tiny proportion of the armaments being brought to bear.

It was hard to make out the coastline from here, but it seemed the fighting had moved too close to the coastline to be safe for the larger ships.

"They're trying to land," Henely said without looking away from his spyglass. "Some of them may already have succeeded."

One ship in particular was ablaze. Its sails acting as chaff and spreading cinders and light across the area. She could see they had run it up onto the beach and abandoned it. It was not a good sign.

If the Jeranonian fleet was in enough trouble that westerners were already making landfall, they might already be too late.

The Kingfisher was running silent now. The sailors in the rigging above making whatever adjustments they'd needed to follow the captain's orders. All the lanterns had been doused as well, and the only light came from a waning moon and the fires of doomed ships ahead. When they were perhaps a mile out from the nearest vessels, Henely nodded slightly without taking his eyes from the spyglass. The captain was scowling at whatever he saw, but looked determined, not defeated.

"There's a knot of eight ships on this flank of the battle. Looks like three of ours and five of theirs. We're going to even those odds while they're distracted by the fight."

He handed her the spyglass, and Johanna gasped as she raised it to her eye.

All eight ships were grappled together in a tangle with two Jeranonian ships at the centre. All five of the western vessels had surrounded them while another Jeranonian ship had come to their aid and was boarding from the far side. One of the western ships was on fire, but the fighting on deck at the heart of the tangle was fierce. The crews of the two friendly ships only holding on because they'd given up so much ground. If the Kingfisher was going to do something, it had to be now.

Henely took back the spyglass and held up a hand, which Wrigley watched intently.

The distance between them shrunk, the order for silent running making it feel as if the entire crew were holding its breath. She could make out the details now with her own eyes. The western ships were larger than their own, with thicker hulls designed not for speed or style, but for carrying capacity. These were troop transports. A second row of ports below their cannons could be opened to allow oars to be lowered into the water.

Why do I know that?

A quick look at the other ships showed that not all of

them had that feature. She pointed it out to Henely, who nodded.

"You have a good eye. That one will house Augrahl warriors or northmen. Nostahl aren't strong enough to row a ship that size, and Imbic would never design something so uniform."

The Kingfisher sped towards the target at a frightening speed. Three hundred spans, two hundred… When she could make out individuals on the deck of the ship they were racing towards, Johanna became nervous. Surely the captain wasn't going to ram the other ship?

At a little under two hundred spans, the captain said calmly to the helmsman, "Hard to starboard."

The man responded by hauling on the wheel for all he was worth, and the Kingfisher spun, shedding speed as she came about.

Henely leaned against the rail as the ship manoeuvred, and the instant the Kingfisher was in line with the western ship, dropped his hand.

"Fire and reload!" Wrigley called to the men below decks from his place on the main deck. An instant later, Johanna jumped as a series of concussive blasts sounded from below, vibrating the entire ship.

In the last two decades since its discovery, the back powder produced by the herbalists and apothecary's guild in Harverness had changed naval warfare completely. Word was the King was about ready to send in the army and take their secrets by force, sick of their monopoly on such an important tool of war. For the second time in an hour, she wondered where that new tidbit of information had come from. Were they further fragments of memory returning, or just some nonsense she'd imagined? It was hard to draw a line about what was real and what wasn't when you couldn't trust your own recollection. At any rate, wherever the powder came from, whoever had produced it, she had to admit the results were impressive.

Lines of smoke and fire leapt from the Kingfisher's side as her port cannons blasted the western vessel's flank with a dozen steel balls. Wood splintered and shattered across the gap, and several of the shots caused enough damage that their impacts joined to create a sizable tear in the ship's hull. It wasn't enough. The ship was badly damaged, the large hole showing off some of the inner deck and a batch of small casks. Unfortunately, the damage was all above the waterline, and the Kingfisher had moved on, out of alignment for another broadside.

A light appeared on the mid-deck, drawing their attention. A moment later, a single arrow flew from the Kingfisher, penetrating one of the holes the cannon fire had left, and disappearing inside. Aterby put down his bow, satisfied.

Henely frowned, but a moment later a deep boom echoed across the gap and the enemy ship lurched, a gaping hole appearing amidships where the arrow had gone in. Water began rushing into the breach, and in seconds the western ship had tilted to an unusable angle, being held afloat only by its grapples to the two Jeranonian ships.

She looked down at Aterby, dumbfounded. The man just shrugged.

"Small barrels like those are only used for one thing on a warship."

"Powder storage," Henely agreed. "Very nicely done, Private."

Aterby nodded, but the captain had already turned his

attention back to the fight. The other ships had seen them now, but grappled and engaged as they were, only two of the four remaining enemies could do anything about it. The reinforcing Jeranonian ship still blocked the other pair.

"Thirty degrees to port. Keep us moving around their perimeter, but on an angle to give them a broadside without exposing us to the same."

"Aye, Sir," the helmsman replied.

"Now the real fight begins," Henely muttered.

Johanna couldn't help but nod. Their element of surprise had been expended, but used well. Now they had to do as much damage as they could, as quickly as they could, or risk being overwhelmed.

She didn't know what the situation on the other ships was, but at least now it was four on four. They also had a significant tactical advantage, with the Kingfisher not being tied down in the grapple.

"Prepare to fire!" Henely called down to the deck.

The helmsman knew his job, and brought them in at a thirty-degree angle which would allow the cannons on the Kingfisher to all fire before the next enemy ship could respond. Under normal circumstances, the western ship could have pivoted to counter, but tied in place as they were, it was an easy shot.

"Fire!" Henely called again as the Kingfisher came in line with the target. It was a smaller vessel this time, without the ports for oars, but an elaborate figurehead shaped like a pouncing cat painted a garish red.

Wrigley shouted the order down below, and cannon fire ripped from the Kingfisher before the other vessel's crew could respond. For a moment, Johanna was concerned they might damage the Jeranonian ships beyond.

The Kingfisher was a good ship, and fast, but not one of the Jeranonian navy's largest. The single volley from its dozen cannons was once again not quite enough to sink the western nations' ship. It did, however, reduce the enemy cannon deck to splinters.

"Fire at will!" Henely called down to the X.O.

Wrigley nodded and repeated the order for the men below decks.

"Keep us within firing range," he said to the helmsman.

Blast after blast shot from the Kingfisher's cannons as each gun crew reloaded and fired and reloaded again. In minutes, the western ship was damaged beyond repair, out of the fight, and taking on water.

The Kingfisher shuddered. Johanna almost lost her footing as the deck lurched.

Around the edge of the dying ship, the third western vessel had freed itself from the tangle and was coming about as quickly as it could.

"Hard to port!" Henely ordered.

"But sir!" the helmsman got out before the captain reached for the wheel and started the manoeuvre himself.

The helmsman jumped to and helped turn the wheel despite his previous objection, and the Kingfisher wheeled until it was facing the tangle. They had nowhere to go, and no room to turn, but with the enemy ship bearing down, they were about to be engaged anyway.

"Fire everything!" Henely shouted.

There was a moment of hesitation as Wrigley passed down the order, and then chaos as the Kingfisher and the enemy ship fired at once. The Kingfisher's cannons mangled the bow of the westerners' ship badly enough that the water coming in immediately dragged them to port, listing off to the side. But the Kingfisher had taken damage as well. Two of its cannons were gone, blown into the sea by the force of the enemy blast. A large hole now replaced them on that side of the ship.

Henely looked over the rail in alarm, but stood again with a scowl and no comment.

The remaining cannon crews continued to fire, but it was clear already they would not sink the enemy before the westerners could deliver a broadside of their own.

"Take out their cannons! Take out their cannons!" Wrigley was shouting down below, but there wasn't time.

Henely turned to her calmly. A boulder in the storm. "If you're going to do anything, it needs to be now."

They were close enough now that she could see the large grinning face of the Augrahl captain on the other ship. His stretched grey skin and large, pointed teeth giving him a terrifying aspect even without the foot-long curved and polished black horns which adorned the top of his head.

"Aterby, up here," she called.

The ranger rushed over, and she pointed at the Augrahl captain.

"The moment before they are in position to fire their cannons, take him out."

He nodded and nocked an arrow. It would be a matter of seconds.

The Kingfisher's cannoneers were still firing, and having some success, but this ship was a big one, far larger than even the first vessel they'd ambushed. It sported three masts and twenty cannons to a side. It even had one mounted on the bow which they'd already holed the Kingfisher with.

What can I do to stop that?

Johanna frantically thought about all the spells she'd used since waking on the island, about every dream full of half recovered fragments of teaching and lore. There had to be something, some key…

That's it! The key.

She looked back at the enemy ship now with sails unfurled and approaching at full speed. They were almost in range.

She concentrated hard on that bow cannon, desperately trying to form an image in her mind of its aperture sealing. And it worked. Johanna smiled as the tempered steel of the cannon closed over like a scab. She extended the metal as she had with the key, moulding it into her desired shape. That was one. The Kingfisher's cannoneers had taken out five more, but there was no chance she could wreck all the rest in time. Concentrating on the midships cannons, she repeated the spell four more times before the enemy could gain position to fire.

"Brace for impact! Henely shouted.

An instant before the enemy ship was at the correct angle to fire, Aterby loosed his arrow. The Augrahl captain fell out of sight, and the moment passed when he should have ordered the barrage. Then the world exploded around her.

Fragments of wood shattered in every direction. The rail in front of her simply disappeared as it took a direct hit, and Aterby was sent flying backward by a piece of debris. She picked herself up from the deck, arm bleeding from a glancing wound and ears ringing from the concussion of the blasts. But it could have been much worse. The instant of hesitation Aterby's shot had caused meant that half the enemy cannons had missed all together as they overshot their firing position. Only the six at the back had holed the Kingfisher, and those which she'd sabotaged had done more damage to their own ship than hers.

For each cannon she'd closed the end of, a gaping wound now appeared in the enemy flank. She'd only meant for them to stop firing, but this was better.

Henely was up and shouting orders already. She wanted to check on Aterby, but forced herself to focus on her task before the enemy ship could reorient for another volley. She spent the next minute sealing the ends of all their remaining cannons, and when she looked around, Aterby was already being escorted below decks by another sailor. He appeared injured, but not too badly. There would be time to check on him, and thank him, later. The enemy was still coming though, swinging around in a wide arc that was all their damaged bow allowed.

"Hard to port!" she heard Henely yelling. "Protect the starboard flank! Get us some room to manoeuvre! X.O., Damage report!"

"Whatever you do, Captain, keep us on their damaged side. I've sealed the rest of the cannons there, and the big one at the bow. They'll explode if they try to use them. Their port side is still operational though."

Henely nodded intently. "Thank you, you may have just saved all our lives."

Johanna felt her lips twitch, but it wasn't a grin. "Let's just get this done."

Wrigley appeared from the ladder, and his report was not encouraging.

"We're down to four cannons on the starboard side, and the hull has sustained significant damage aft of midships, but for now we're not taking on water."

"Still in the fight, then," Henely said with a frown.

"Aye, Sir, but we'll need to be careful about exposing our starboard flank. Another volley like that in the right spot could crack the hull like an egg."

"Noted," Henely replied.

Wrigley gave a sharp salute and returned to his own duties.

"They're coming around!" the helmsman called.

The enemy ship had almost completed its turn and was now beginning the short run back to their position. They were damaged heavily on their starboard side, but still had most of the cannons on the aft half of the hull in working condition, or so they thought. What she'd done wasn't visible to the crews inside the ship.

"Expose our starboard side to them," Johanna said without thinking. "Let them come in for the kill, but make sure they pass with their starboard side facing us. We have to get them to fire those cannons."

Henely looked at her for a moment, weighing her up. She could see it in his eyes. If he trusted her now, and she was wrong, his ship and crew were dead.

"How sure are you?" he asked.

"You saw those large holes amidships?" she responded instead.

Henely nodded that he had.

"That sure," Johanna replied. "That was their own ordinance backfiring, not ours hitting."

Henely's hand went white as he balled them into fists and made his decision.

"Rig for running!" he called down to Wrigley.

"Sir?" the X.O. replied. For a long moment, Johanna wasn't sure he was going to follow the order.

"Now, Commander, we have a plan."

Wrigley looked dubious, but gave a half-hearted 'Aye Sir' before going about his tasks.

Johanna was fairly sure he didn't believe there was a plan at all, and would mutiny within minutes if one didn't appear. The man just wasn't about to run out on the fight, no matter what. She might have even admired him for it if she thought it was loyalty rather than pig-headed stubbornness driving him. The enemy ship was driving through the water at them as fast as its broken bow would allow, and Henely ordered the helmsman to come about.

"I want you to cross that ship's path and flee into open water. Put our damaged side towards the enemy momentarily, but continue the turn. Either they'll shoot at us and cripple themselves, or they'll be forced to chase us, leaving the Kingfisher's undamaged section on their exposed starboard side.

The helmsman shook his head even while turning the wheel. It was going to be close.

The western ship was bearing down on them, less than a hundred spans away now, and coming fast.

Johanna watched in seeming slow motion as they sailed into its route, and then crossed in front with agonising slowness. They would make it. Barely.

As they passed the enormous ship's bow, a wave of cannon fire ripped at it from the other side. The force of it pushed the whole craft further away from the tangle, and back onto a collision course. That fire had to have come from one of the Jeranonian vessels at the centre of the tangle. It didn't matter. It hadn't helped. The ship was barely fifty spans away now, and it would not miss.

"No! Helmsman, hard to starboard! Brace! Brace! Brace!" Henely yelled as he grabbed for the mizzenmast.

The helmsman spun the wheel, but it was too little, too late.

Johanna was thrown to the deck as the western ship clipped their aft section. The Kingfisher was jolted hard enough to tear a chunk out of its side as the two vessels glanced off each other.

The deck heaved, and she slid towards the edge. Henely's outstretched hand was the only thing that stopped her going overboard as the ship bucked at the impact.

They didn't capsize though, and with a lurch back in the other direction, the Kingfisher righted itself.

"Fire now!" Henely shouted.

Instead of a curved course that would have seen their undamaged port side facing the enemy ship, the collision had knocked them about far enough that their entire starboard was now in line with the enemy. Both ships had their damaged sections towards each other as they passed, but the western ship had far more cannons still pointing from their emplacements. Johanna grimaced. If even a few of those shots got through it was over.

There was a huge barrage of sound and light, and wooden debris flew in every direction. Johanna ducked her head, still prone on the deck, and tried not to give in to panic. This was madness. Madness accompanied by cheering...

She looked up and saw the western vessel crumpling into the water, its entire starboard hull peeled away like an apple skin. The Kingfisher was still taking shots at it, sending it on its way, but the damage was done.

"Bring us in and grapple to the Harbinger! Prepare for boarding!"

Johanna just looked at the captain as she knelt and then stood. They'd sunk three enemy vessels already, but there were still two engaged in hand to hand fighting with the three Jeranonian ships just in this tangle. Beyond them, dozens more vessels from both sides continued to slug it out in the darkness, both with cannons and on deck.

Despite the men's cheers, this battle was far from over.

'Individuals born with mutations so severe that the individual cannot communicate are fit only for the battlefield.'
Excerpt from the Imbic 'Book of Continuance'.

CHAPTER 17

STEEL IN MOONLIGHT

"Throw grapples!" Wrigley shouted, and across the Kingfisher, twenty or more sailors spun up metal claws attached to ropes and swung them across the small gap between the ships.

Archers were already stationed on the fore and afterdecks. Between their covering fire and the few remaining Jeranonian sailors still fighting across the two ship decks, the Kingfisher was joined to the tangle without further casualties.

The sailors pulled the ropes tight, and the moment they were at rest, the entire crew of the Kingfisher were leaping over the rails and onto the deck of the beleaguered Harbinger. The men Johanna had somehow wound up in command of joined them.

The ship was of the same design as the Kingfisher, and their decks were at similar height, making for an easy transition for the attackers.

With fifty fresh sailors and rangers entering the fight, the remaining Nostahl and Augrahl were overwhelmed and disposed of in moments. It seemed they'd been just as worn down as the crews from the two Jeranonian ships they were violently assaulting.

"Did they make it below decks?" Wrigley asked a lieutenant as soon as the deck was clear. They were near enough that Johanna could hear the conversation from her place on the Kingfisher. Only she, Henely, and the helmsman remained on board.

"Yes, sir, might be some still down there," the young man replied.

There were several tears and slashes in his uniform, and he swayed on his feet.

"Take a seat lieutenant, you've done well, but we've got it from here."

He seemed about to object, but could barely stand. The realisation that he was no longer in imminent danger of dying the moment he let down his guard sapped what little adrenaline he'd been running on. He followed the order without acknowledging it, and the way he half collapsed, hands trembling on the hilt of his sword, Johanna was not sure the movement had been intentional.

Wrigley had already moved on.

"Beta shift, secure the deck. Rangers, sweep below decks from aft, alpha shift, you're with me!"

Millard nodded, though not part of the Kingfisher's command, and took his men to the aft hatch. Aterby was nowhere to be seen. She wanted to head below to check on his injury, heal it if she could. Until the rest of the crew returned to the deck of the Harbinger victorious, she didn't dare.

There was still fighting on the other ships, but the sailors left on deck were not crossing just yet. The Harbinger wasn't just grappled to the second Jeranonian ship, but to a western vessel at its bow as well. It would do no one any good if the men below decks returned to find themselves behind enemy lines. It was hard to watch the fighting without intervening, to see the men struggling to stay alive a few desperate moments longer. But it was necessary if the overall mission were to be accomplished.

It seemed an eternity until the first sailor returned to the deck, but was probably only a few minutes. Johanna felt helpless waiting. She wasn't a battlemage, that much she was certain of, but there had to be something more she could do.

Behind the sailor, a flood of men came pouring out of the hatches, and Wrigley turned to face them.

"Harbinger secure, Sir. Moving on," he called across the deck.

"Good hunting, Mr. Wrigley," Henely called back.

The X.O. saluted, and another minute passed while the survivors, which seemed to include most of their men, prepared to board the second ship.

The moment they were set, Wrigley gave the order. A wave of bodies swept over the rails, joining the two Jeranonian ships and clashed with the remaining western crew.

On the far side of the fight, a cheer went up. Johanna looked across to where she could see one of the western ships now swarming with Jeranonian sailors. The crew of the ship which had come in to help its two besieged colleagues, grappling the westerners from the other side of the tangle, had apparently won their fight. Without waiting, they swarmed over onto the final western ship and soon disappeared below decks after taking care of the few Nostahl left there in defence. Most of the far larger and stronger Augrahl troops had been committed to attack the other ships, and they were now spread too thin. What the westerners had expected to be an easy five-on-two victory had soured with both the reinforcing Jeranonian ship, and then the Kingfisher creating chaos on their flanks. With their tactical advantage lost, the odds had turned now, and despite their diminished strength, the remaining Jeranonian forces were firmly in command. With both the final western and Jeranonian ships now under assault by the King's forces, it was only a matter of time until this was resolved.

"I'm going below to treat the wounded," she told the captain.

Henely looked around for an instant, surveying the situation, before nodding.

Without further conversation, she left the afterdeck and headed through the narrow hatch that led inside the ship. Down in the crew quarters, hammocks lined the walls. Most were empty, but a few contained bandaged men whom the ship's medic had already seen to.

She went down the line. None of these men looked too bad, and none of them were Aterby. Yes, they were all injured, but none of it looked life-threatening. The worst cases would be in the undersized infirmary further into the ship. As she approached the stern, the sound of moaning became louder, as well as the voice of the medic insisting that someone hold a patient down. She pushed open the door and walked through the hatch.

The infirmary was full. Besides the medic and an assistant, there were six other men in the room. Aterby was sitting on the floor, clutching his stomach. The medic was busy with another sailor, whose right thigh sported a puncture wound caused by flying debris, a large piece of which was still embedded. He was bleeding heavily onto the deck, and wouldn't last long.

"Move aside," she ordered.

The medic looked up, about to protest. When he saw who had given the order, to his credit, he didn't hesitate.

Johanna rammed the delving spell into the wound and immediately found the problem. The main vein in his leg had been severed, and only the force of the wood penetrating his flesh had stopped it flowing until now. She began joining the flesh together until the vein was long enough to reach the other side.

"Take it out," she said to the medic. The man and his assistant did a fair job of removing the debris without causing further damage. Even as the blood flow increased from his body, she fused the two sides of the vein together, stopping the fluid loss in its tracks.

From there, it was a matter of joining the flesh as she had many times now, while the medic just looked on with an envious expression on his face.

When she was finished, the sailor lay unconscious from blood loss. That wasn't something she knew how to fix, or at least, she didn't think she did. The rest of his recovery would just have to be up to his own body and constitution.

She moved over to Aterby, who was sweaty and slumped against a wall.

"I think he's bleeding internally," the medic said. "But without knowing where, I'd do more harm than good opening him up. If you can do more, please do so."

He was already washing his hands in a bucket of water so he could move on to the next patient.

Aterby was barely responsive, so she laid him down on the deck, causing the tall man to grunt in pain. She used the delving spell again, but was unsure what to look for. His pelvis was cracked, that she fixed in moments, but there must be something else. He was holding his gut, not his hips. It took her a long moment, but she found a tear in one of his organs. What it was called she couldn't say, but the damage was obvious once she located it. Fixing the injury was tricky since she had no direct line of sight, and had to rely solely on the feel of the delving to guide her. Unlike his pelvic bone, which remained in position throughout, the organ shifted every time she tried to manipulate it. It was like trying to pick up a marble with two other marbles. The ship rocked slightly on a wave, and she took a deep breath, calming herself and completing the work. By the time the damage was healed, Aterby was asleep or unconscious, but he was breathing normally, and his face was no longer contorted in pain.

"He's obviously your friend, but we could use your help over here," the medic said from behind her.

Johanna stood. She had a feeling she'd be here for a while.

*   *   *

For the next hour, she went from ship to ship, healing the most critical cases until Captain Henely called her back. The last of the western forces had been dispatched while she'd been below, and the captain had been conferring with the officers acting as captains of the other three ships since then.

It was midnight by the time the ships separated, throwing off their grapples from each other's railings. The remnants of the two western ships the Kingfisher had sunk early in the battle had long since been dealt with, and were now resting on the seabed below.

A mile to the west, the battle raged on. There was too much chaos to tell who was winning right now, but one thing was clear, the western fleet's massive flagship was wreaking havoc on their forces. Even from here, in the darkness, she could see its double row of cannons firing. The monstrous vessel sported fifty to a side, and an iron ram. Four masts rose from its hull, and a ballista for fouling the rigging of other ships was mounted on each side of the deck. Slots for oars at irregular intervals dotted the lower hull.

It was a ship designed to kill other ships. It had no other purpose.

As it turned out, Henely was the most senior commander left in their group, and the plan he presented was simple. Take every ship they had around the edge of the fight and blow that monstrosity out of the water.

They couldn't win a boarding action with the men they had left, so he'd ordered skeleton crews aboard every ship along with a full complement of gunners. Between the remnants of the four crews, they had enough men for the mission, but once the two captured western vessels were included, it was a close thing. From now until the battle was decided, every man would have to stand his post.

Johanna had returned to her place beside Henely on the afterdeck, and the night was still for several moments as the two captured vessels passed them by. His idea was to make it look as though the Jeranonian ships were in pursuit. If it worked, the flagship might ignore, or even move to protect the two decoys. Hopefully for long enough that they could get into position to fire a clear volley before the enemy realised what had happened.

The Harbinger led the chase, still having an intact hull. The Ravager and Stormfront followed close behind. Henely had ordered Wrigley to take command of the latter as its officers had all died during the fighting. The Kingfisher, with its damaged hull, brought up the rear.

It was a bold move, and not necessarily one they should have made. But with most of the fleet now in close combat, there was little they could do on that front. The fighting in the tangle of surrounded ships had been fierce, and they were down to less than two full crews between the four Jeranonian vessels. So it was this, or distil their crews and abandon four of the ships to add to the chaos at the centre of the fight in yet another boarding action. That wouldn't turn the tide. This might.

The two western ships sped up, and with it their escorts. It was all the Kingfisher could do to keep up with the damage to its hull.

They tacked north, then headed west around the outskirts of the battle, bypassing grappled ships and the wrecked hulls of the vessels which had come off worst. Several were still in flames, and bodies floated everywhere amongst the debris. Some were still desperately trying to swim to safety, hundreds more were simply floating.

Johanna became ever more nervous as the seconds wore by. If the western flagship had looked huge before, it was monstrous now.

As they rounded a final pair of grappled ships, both abandoned as one side or the other had been victorious and moved on, they began the southbound leg.

As she watched, the flagship delivered a crushing blow to a Jeranonian frigate, every one of its fifty port cannons firing a broadside into the far smaller ship.

With a splitting of wood audible even from here, the frigate broke in two as the force of the blasts knocked it on its side. The hull was shredded, and more than one shot made it all the way through. The breaches on either side gave the ocean every conceivable way to take hold and consume it in mere moments.

She felt herself staring in shock, her expression mirrored on Henely's face as he shook his head to clear it.

"X.O. Pass the word, when the time comes, fire everything at the waterline of that ship. We can't get into a slugging match with it."

The new first officer, whose name she didn't know, called back and 'Aye, Sir,' but seemed nervous.

He had every right to be.

The lead captured ship was approaching now, and someone on the flagship seemed to have noticed. The ship began a leisurely turn to starboard, intending to bring its cannons to bear on the four ships pursuing the western vessels.

"Here we go," Henely muttered just loudly enough for her to hear. "Once the fighting starts, don't wait for specific orders. Do whatever you can to help please, Mage Johanna."

She glanced at his worried expression, but he didn't look away from the massive ship whose cannons were nearly in range.

The first decoy ship trimmed its sails and swung hard to port right in front of the behemoth, followed closely by the second. By the time it had made the turn, the first ship was firing, attempting to take out the lower row of cannons.

The surprise was complete, and Johanna breathed a slight sigh of relief as a dozen of its emplacements disappeared in gouts of smoke and flame. It was a stunning blow, but not a fatal one. The ship sailed on, trying to pass by before the enemy could regroup and fire with the thirty plus cannons still in operation.

They made it, but the following vessel wasn't so lucky.

The flagship fired a broadside as it passed, and despite the captured western vessel getting off shots of its own, it was far from an even fight.

Its main mast was blown clear off the boat as a cannon shot hit it directly, causing the sails to collapse and the mast to drag down into the water. The few sailors who weren't thrown from the rigging began desperately trying to cut ropes and release the ruined mast from the tangle of sheets. If they couldn't do it soon, the drag from the ocean would capsize the ship. Whether or not they succeeded, they could no longer manoeuvre, putting them out of the fight.

The captured ship continued listing to port as it coasted on by. Large holes were visible in the deck, and the starboard hull facing the flagship must be much worse. Yet they'd managed at least one good hit near the waterline, and a few more along the lower cannon bank. It wasn't enough.

The gigantic ship began swinging to port, attempting to hide its damaged side from the four approaching Jeranonian vessels. Harbinger changed course and rounded their bow before they could complete the turn, but whatever happened next was obscured as the small vessel was hidden behind the massive ship's flank.

Cannon fire sounded, but there was no telling whether the flagship had been further damaged, or if the Harbinger had even survived.

Ahead of them, Stormfront and Ravager split, one to port, the other to starboard. Their timing was impeccable, and the broadside the flagship fired at them from the undamaged starboard cannons largely missed. There were a few glancing blows, and a direct hit to one of Ravager's cannons sent the heavy gun tumbling into the ocean. The two ships ignored the light damage, and a moment later opened up with salvos of their own. Wood shrieked on the enemy ship, and a large tear appeared near the waterline amidships.

Henely nodded.

"X.O. order the gunners to target that breach!" he called.

The cannon fire had not ceased, but whatever was happening with the captured ship and Harbinger on the other side of the flagship was anybody's guess.

She said a quick prayer to the Maker for them, and then it was their turn.

The Kingfisher swung to starboard, keeping its damaged side away from the hulking enemy ship, and fired a salvo of its own. Several of the cannons hit their target, opening the breach in the enemy hull wider. Johanna did her best to sabotage some of their cannons like she had before, but there were too many. The warship began turning again, and it was clear the Kingfisher was its target.

"Hard to starboard! Put them astern and reduce our aspect!" Henely called to the helmsman, who was happy to oblige.

The Kingfisher was a good ship, but she was also damaged, and the manoeuvre took longer than it should. Before they could fully turn away, the stern erupted in a series of blows that caused the deck to buck like a horse.

Johanna was thrown flat against the deck, hitting her head against the hard wood. She did her best to shake it off, and when she could focus, it was to find timbers once sanded and polished to a fine finish lying warped and cracked where they had not been blown clear off the boat. Beside her, Henely lay dead, a foot-long shard of decking having pierced his neck.

She looked around in a daze. The ship seemed to be on an odd angle, and her ears were making a high-pitched whining that drowned out almost everything else.

The new X.O. rushed past her without checking to see if she was all right. He leant down over the shattered remnant of the stern and punched the deck. He stood and gave the enemy flagship a severe scowl before his shoulders slumped.

"All hands abandon ship! Pass the word below decks and prepare the lifeboat!"

There was a moment of silence at the drastic orders, then men began running to obey.

"We can't leave," Johanna said as the man came back and helped her to her feet. "We can't see what the other ships are doing from here, we could be the last ones left."

The man shrugged. "Doesn't matter, this ship is going down. We've got maybe two minutes at the rate we're taking on water."

"Doesn't matter?!" Johanna demanded, pulling away from the man's grip. "We're fighting for our lives, and it doesn't matter to you that we're going to lose the ship?"

The man halted and looked at her nonplussed. "It's not that I don't care, it's that I can't do anything about it. The Kingfisher is going down no matter what I do, and it is my duty now to get the crew to safety."

Johanna wanted to argue that they couldn't give up, that they had to keep fighting. Where that impulse came from she wasn't sure. Was it a result of stress the battle had placed on all of them, or some relic of her previous life? One thing was certain; if they didn't get off the ship soon, she would never have the chance to find out.

This man was only a lieutenant. She outranked him. She could order him to stay. Except that she found she couldn't.

"Get your crew to the lifeboat, Captain," she told him instead. The man nodded and left. She followed him down the ladder to the main deck. A kicked ant's nest of activity was occurring as the sailors and soldiers attempted to lower the boat from its out-of-kilter moorings. It wouldn't be big enough for all of them, but it was sturdy. Some of the men could swim along at its sides long enough to be picked up by a friendly vessel. Assuming they could take the behemoth of a warship down.

She stood next to the helmsman, who hadn't left his post at the wheel despite the disaster unfolding around him.

"You should get to the boat," she said as the men lowered it over the side.

"Begging you pardon, Mage, but I have no intention of joining the others."

Johanna just looked at him for a long moment.

"What's your plan?" she asked. The man didn't seem suicidal, he appeared more focused than anything else.

"The lieutenant says the ship's lost. I accept that, but I won't have her go down for nothing. The stern's damaged, but they missed the rudder, and the bow's fine. I can work with that."

Johanna just looked at him. "You're going to ram it?" she demanded.

The man shrugged. "They've already got significant damage amidships. If I can ram the Kingfisher into the breach hard enough, she might just get stuck and take that monster down with her when she goes."

"Will you be able to get up to speed with that much water dragging at the stern?"

The helmsman shrugged again. "Maybe with your help," he suggested.

She wanted her memories back, wanted to return home, wanted to return the small cat statue and rings which still sat in her buttoned pocket. None of that would happen though unless they won this battle. And for that to happen, the enemy flagship had to die.

Johanna nodded.

"Come on you two!" the lieutenant called. The officer was now alone on the deck by the port rail. She hadn't seen Aterby, Mick, or Millard head over the rail, but she trusted the lieutenant not to leave anyone behind. The man had taken to his new responsibilities well.

"We're staying. You go. Get our men to safety. Maker willing, we'll see you when it's done," Johanna called back.

The lieutenant seemed about to argue, but then shook his head. She outranked him and they both knew it.

"When it's done," he repeated, and climbed down over the rail.

Johanna gave them a ten second count and then turned to the helmsman.

"Hard to port. I'll be below."

"Yes, Ma'am," the helmsman replied with an intense grin, and turned to his work.

All things end. All things begin.
Common arborii saying

CHAPTER 18

THE PRICE OF PASSAGE

Johanna went below through the aft hatch, the ship tilting as the helmsman swung them about. She went a few feet down the corridor and headed down a deck via a ladder bolted into a wall. As she reached the deck below, her feet splashed into salty water, and it disturbed her to find the ocean had already claimed the Kingfisher up to her knees. She headed aft, sloshing down the passage with purpose. She didn't think she'd be trapped down here. If she could make it to the stern of the ship, she imagined she could swim out through a hole in the hull if need be. She hadn't seen the damage with her own eyes, but the lieutenant's reaction had told her all she needed to know.

There was a hatch in her way. Johanna pulled on it, but the built-up weight of the water made it impossible to move. She concentrated on the hinges for a long moment, changing their shape until the pins fell out, then did the same with the strip of wood against the frame. It took some time, but eventually the door fell inwards now that it was too small for the space.

What it revealed left her more chilled than the water now up past her knees.

The entire rear of the ship was missing. Jagged timbers

simply ended, and the ocean and starlit sky provided a vista that would have been the envy of any window.

What can I possibly do to fix this?

We only need a minute. Think of something, she chided herself.

She clambered over the door and entered what remained of the chamber. The deck was on a slant towards the breach this far to the stern. The ocean pulling hard at the wooden construction which had defied its grasp since the day it set sail.

She'd expected that. What stunned her was the sight of Aterby strapped to a table at the edge of the room just shy of the destruction. Forgetting what she was here for, she rushed over to the table and loosened the straps, cursing the fool of a lieutenant for not seeing to the evacuation properly. How many others were still down here? Aterby was pale, his lips blue, and something had hit him hard on the head. She pushed into his flesh with a delving spell, and stopped. His heart was still, his skull cracked, and several internal organs were crushed beyond repair from the impact of something extremely heavy falling on his rib cage.

She sat down in the chilling water pooling around her legs and sobbed. Aterby had been a rock, always willing to go the extra mile, to put himself in danger for the group. For him to meet his end while lying in a recovery bed was just unfair.

He hadn't been hit directly, but it seemed that one of the enemy cannon shots had torn through the hull, expending its momentum and then falling or rolling onto him. Whatever the cause, that last volley from the enemy flagship had killed him, and she intended to return that favour.

She stood, pulling herself up out of the water and moving back to the table where Aterby lay.

"Sorry," she whispered, moving a lock of hair away from his eyes. She just didn't have the words to express herself any better than that in this moment.

With a last grimace of regret, she turned her back on his body and moved to the very edge of the decking. It was hard to tell where it ended. The darkness outside made the ocean swirling through the cabin all but black, but she thought she was close.

But what could she do? The Kingfisher continued to take on water, adding weight to the boat's mass, pushing down the stern while no doubt lifting the bow slightly out of the water. That would work to their advantage if they could get there. Extra height at the impact site would help them breach the enemy flagship and wedge the Kingfisher into the wound on its starboard hull as it sank.

The problem was speed. The Kingfisher's masts were intact, but all the extra water churning into the breach was weighing them down, and slowing the ship in the process. That was what she needed to fix.

For an instant she considered trying to extend the planks and fix the hull, but that spell was slow even to form a key. There wasn't time. Could she push the water out somehow? It seemed a longshot, and she'd never had any control of the shield spell that had saved her life on two occasions now since waking on the island. It was pure reflex that made that one work, and unavailable to her right now. But what if there was a way to kill two birds with one stone? What if she could push the water out and increase their speed at the same time?

She didn't even need to imagine a way to make it

happen, it was so obvious. Wind. The ship was designed to be propelled by wind, and wind would serve her here. If she could force it to do her bidding.

She reached out a hand, imagining the wind changing direction at that point. She felt the air stir, but it was just a breeze. The now familiar click in her mind had not yet occurred. She took a deep breath. They must be closing with the flagship by now.

Her aching left hand joined her right, and she closed her eyes, imagining the air rushing from her fingertips to the water still sloshing into the back of the ship. It had reached her thighs now, and seemed to be speeding up. When she had the image firmly in mind, she opened her eyes and felt the familiar click that she now recognised as her mind accessing the Gift.

For the first few seconds, debris flew around the cabin, but then it cleared as the sudden gale in the room cleared everything through the breach. The water was being dented by the force of the spell, but that was all. She concentrated, doing her best to increase its speed, but she was constrained by the need for more air to rush in and replace what she was forcing out. She needed more air. With a minute shrug, she imagined the sides of the room exploding outward, and with no more warning than that it happened. A foot wide hole appeared to either side of her as debris once again swirled around the room, cutting her face and arm before it cleared the breach. She tried to ignore the stinging pain, but the salt spray made that difficult. She took another deep breath. Pain or no pain, she had work to do. She reimagined the air spell so that it came in from the holes she had just made, and was forced out against the water and through the rear breach.

It worked. The spell was already five times more powerful than it had been, and the water was now being shoved out of the ship as fast as it could enter.

I can do more.

Focusing on the currents of air she was manipulating, she pushed them harder against the water, churning the surface to froth as the deck behind her cleared of water. With some of the weight gone, the Kingfisher seemed to pick up speed on its own, sailing more smoothly as it had before being damaged.

I can do more.

With every shred of focus she could bring to bear, she pushed the air to move faster, to hit the water with more force. She kept hitting it in a continuous stream.

Maybe it was her imagination, but she thought the Kingfisher was picking up speed.

"Whatever you're doing down there, keep it up!" a faint voice reached her from the main deck.

Johanna pushed the air harder, though at this speed it was hard to keep the spell in check. She somehow knew that if she doubted herself now, if she imagined the spell failing, or worse, running amok, that was exactly what would eventuate.

She bit down on her tongue to focus herself and kept herself firmly on task.

A vast shudder ran through the ship, accompanied by the sound of explosions.

She almost lost control, but they were still moving, still coursing through the water. That hadn't been them ramming the flagship, it must have been another volley of fire aimed their way.

Good, she thought. If they were bothering to waste time

on a ship as crippled as Kingfisher now was, then they must still be a threat. They must be close.

"Brace for impact!" the helmsman's voice sounded distantly.

For a terrified instant Johanna waited for the contact, but a second passed, then another, then…

The world twisted, and Johanna was thrown through the air. The shield spell sprang into being around her without conscious thought and the sphere bounced off the cabin wall. She rolled clear through the breach at the rear of the ship into the ocean beyond, and as she hit the inky black water, she began to sink. Fast.

She couldn't swim in her bubble shield, there was no contact with the water, but her weight remained the same, dragging her towards the seabed. She took a deep breath and cancelled the spell. The ocean came crushing in and it was all she could do to keep herself oriented the correct way to swim upwards in the dim light. Up and up she swam, breaking the surface only when her lungs were burning and her mind beginning to panic.

For long seconds she treaded water, gasping as her heart slowly returned to a more normal pace. Behind her, the Kingfisher was firmly wedged into the damaged section of the flagship.

The whole front end of the Kingfisher was wrecked. But it had lasted long enough to tear its way through the enemy hull, causing the monstrous ship to list towards her due to the extra, poorly distributed weight.

Something hit the water beside her. An arrow! Then another.

She dived below the surface, hiding herself from view, but arrows continued to pour into the ocean around her.

The shield spell was useless to her right now, that much was clear. She wasn't going to make it back to the cover of the Kingfisher's failing hull before she had to resurface though. She looked around underwater, not sure what she was expecting to see. Certainly not the shark at the very depth of her vision. She started for an instant, almost losing her breath before realising the huge fish had no particular interest in her. But still. She redoubled her efforts, but it wasn't enough. Her breath was running out, and she was going to have to risk resurfacing. She was about to change direction when it hit her.

If I can do it with air, maybe I can do it with water as well.

She concentrated, knowing she had only seconds to make this work. She pointed her hands behind her and used the same spell she'd forced the air currents away with, only now using the water around her instead, and propelling herself through the water. For a wonder it worked, though a little too well as she shot up to the surface and skimmed along the waves far faster than she ever could have swum. Plumes of water extended out with force from her outstretched hands, and she shot into the breach at the rear of the Kingfisher as a volley of arrows chased her inside. None found their mark. She cancelled the spell as she reached cover, but she'd misjudged her speed, and crashed into the far wall with bone jarring force. Her arm had healed well since the incident with the Imbic mutation. It had been hurt badly, but not broken as it turned out. She was pretty sure that was no longer the case.

A shadow appeared in the doorway and the Kingfisher's helmsman limped in.

"You're alive!" he exclaimed. "When you didn't answer

I feared the worst."

"Just busy getting back on board without getting shot,"

He looked at her quizzically for a moment, then his eyebrows raised. He pointed at the breach.

She nodded.

"Sorry about that. Can we get out that way?"

"Maybe," she replied. "They know I'm a mage now, so they're going to be watching. I might be able to get us back to the lifeboat, but it's a risk. If anything goes wrong, or the spell doesn't support your weight, we'll be exposed. Even if everything goes right, we'll be in range of their cannons for some time."

"Well," he said eventually. "We can't stay here."

She grimaced. They certainly couldn't. The water was already back up to her thighs as the Kingfisher rode ever lower in the water. She presumed it was taking water from the bow now as well due to both the second enemy volley, and ramming the flagship head on.

"How much damage did we do?" she asked, putting off risking both their lives for another few seconds.

"A lot. Maybe enough. They're taking on water, but it's not a quick process. Their cannons will still be a problem for some time, but they should be all but unable to manoeuvre with us stuck in their side at cross angles like this."

Johanna grinned, but wasn't sure why. She didn't think she was the kind of person to take pleasure in the death of another, even if it was an enemy. If the flagship went down, they'd just killed hundreds.

"Let's get out of here," she said, moving over to Aterby's still strapped down form and placing a gentle hand on the dead man's shoulder.

"Thank you," she whispered.

She sloshed back over to the helmsman who cocked his head in the obvious question.

She shook her head once. There was nothing to be done. He nodded his acceptance and came to meet her.

"What do you need me to do?" he asked.

Johanna grinned slightly. "Just hold on as tightly as you can. If you fall off, I'm not sure I have enough control over this spell yet to come back and get you. To say nothing of finding you in the dark."

"I see?" he replied, though that was clearly not the case.

"Just stand behind me and put your arms around my waist."

He raised an amused eyebrow, and she couldn't help but laugh.

"Don't get any ideas, sailor boy," she said with mock seriousness.

"No, Ma'am. Wouldn't dream of it."

She could hear the playfulness in his voice, but also the respect.

"Best not," she replied in a similar tone as he came to stand behind her.

She gasped as his arm jostled her own, and he let go immediately.

"You're injured!"

"Fairly sure my arm's broken," she agreed. "Doesn't change what we have to do."

"One moment," he said, moving to a cupboard on the upper wall which had survived the bombardment.

"This was the sick bay after all," he said as he returned with a length of bandage and a large triangle piece of fabric. She watched as he gently bound her lower arm and strapped it up against her chest with the fabric sling. He tied a second length around her to keep the sling next to her body and prevent it being jostled.

"I'm Johanna," she said while he worked.

"Michael," the helmsman replied, glancing her way.

When the dressings were secured, he surveyed his work and nodded. "Best I can do right now."

"Thanks," she replied. Her arm hurt from being restrained in the sling, but it would be better in the long term to keep it like that while they moved.

"All right," she said. "Hold on tight."

Michael moved around the dark compartment until he was behind her again. He put his arms around her waist, avoiding her broken arm. Together they waded deeper into the cold, salty water until they were almost at the end of the broken deck.

Johanna concentrated. She only had one arm to force the water away from her this time, but did that actually make any difference? It wasn't like she was paddling with her hands. Could she steer with just one hand? Would it be better to focus the spell on her feet?

She looked out from the destroyed stern of the Kingfisher and thought she could make out its lifeboat in the distance. If she was right, the rest of the Kingfisher's crew were out of cannon range, safe for now, but rowing against the tide to keep it that way.

She leaned into the water and tried to replicate the spell she'd used a minute before.

The click in her mind came easier now, and with only the need to concentrate, she forced the water out behind them with the Gift.

Michael yelped and almost lost his grip as she launched

them out of the ship's rear end, using her good hand to steer the spell like a rudder.

A volley of arrows shot out after them. The slight delay between their emergence from the Kingfisher's hull and the reaction time of the archers firing was enough to get them clear. Anyone attempting to swim at a normal speed would have been shot down in seconds.

A thunderous volley of cannon fire followed, and all around them splashes appeared where the metal balls impacted the ocean.

If just one of those hit…

She weaved left and right across the starlit swell, using her good hand to steer. A cannonball thumped into the water right in front of them and Johanna hesitated for an instant as they shot through the plume of water it left behind. She almost lost control of the spell, but bit down on her tongue and forced herself to concentrate, keeping them just above the surface of the waves until they were no longer in range. The guns on the flagship fell silent, but she could feel their hateful stare on the back of her neck as they made good their escape.

Johanna skimmed them across the ocean surface until they were away, gliding across the wave tops like a pair of dolphins frolicking in the moonlight. The spell meant they never needed to dive though, and soon enough they were approaching the lifeboat.

She reduced the spell's power, and when they were within a dozen spans, let it fade altogether. She felt Michael let go as they slowed enough to fall into the water, and her arm took a jolt as they re-entered. A half-dozen sailors who were already in the water swam over to meet them, and escort them the last stretch to the boat.

"She's injured, get her on board," Michael announced as they arrived.

The sailors helped her paddle the rest of the way, which she was thankful for with one arm strapped to her chest. Soon enough Millard was hauling her over the side with Mick's help.

She rolled and sat clumsily on what turned out to be a rather hard wooden bench, one of several that crossed the width of the lifeboat. The craft was sitting low in the water to the point that the captain had ordered several men to take turns swimming by its side. They would need to be picked up soon.

She looked back at the enemy flagship as they brought Michael on board. Another sailor was ordered to take a turn in the water to make up the difference.

The enormous enemy ship was burning now, but not from anything they'd done. Its far side was billowing smoke, and cannon fire still sounded from the other side of the fight.

The Kingfisher was like a knife in its gut, taking on water more quickly now. The extra weight caused the behemoth to list wildly to starboard as it dragged on the flagship's flank. More importantly, the breach they had caused in the enemy hull was allowing water to enter the flagship there as well. Even better, the angle of list the enemy ship was now on would prevent its port cannons from firing on a level plain. Any Jeranonian ships still operational but out of sight of their lifeboat should be safe enough for now.

The Kingfisher was on a forty-five-degree angle now, its entire stern submerged as it dragged on the larger ship's hull. If this kept up, it would cause the massive gunship to roll soon, and maybe capsize.

There was a crack of wood loud enough to turn every head for a mile in any direction as the Kingfisher broke free. The pressure of its weight releasing tore the enemy hull to shreds. With a cauldron of bubbles it collapsed and submerged as the flagship sprang wildly to port, to level and beyond, then back again. The vast chunk ripped from its side by the Kingfisher's exit allowed the ocean to enter, and it was already sitting lower in the water before it could rock back to upright. More cannon fire sounded from beyond. A lucky hit impacted its main mast, causing it to tilt and foul the rigging of the other masts. The huge beam toppled halfway into the ocean and stopped, stuck on the other sails and dragging the ship like a rudder.

A cheer went up from the men on the boat and Johanna smiled as the flagship sunk even lower in the water. The ships beyond were still firing sporadically. Without a line of sight on the damage the Kingfisher had inflicted, they had no way to know the fight was over. Even if they broke off now, there wasn't enough left of the starboard hull to stop the ocean claiming the vessel in time.

The enormous ship began a wallowing turn to the south, though on purpose or as a result of the half-submerged mast she couldn't tell. A minute passed, and the ship's angle shifted far enough to reveal only two of their own ships still in the fight. In the darkness, it was hard to tell from this far out, but she thought it was the Stormfront and the Ravager. One of their commandeered western ships was engulfed in flames, soon to be taken by the ocean. Of the Harbinger and second western ship there was no sign. They must have been sunk during the fighting.

The first row of enemy cannons dipped below the

waterline, and after a last volley, both the Ravager and Stormfront broke off and left the once mighty vessel to its fate. Stormfront took a course that would bring them back to rescue any survivors from the Kingfisher, while Ravager moved out of cannon range, but stayed in the vicinity to perform the same function there for the other downed vessels.

She looked across at Mick and Millard, abruptly realising that they still didn't know.

"Aterby..." she began.

Millard put a comforting hand on her good shoulder.

"It's okay. They told us."

"Said he never woke up," Mick added sombrely. "Not how he would have wanted to go."

Johanna sighed, there was nothing else to say. They'd both known the man far longer than she had. Anything else at this point would only seem trite.

She turned back to watch the enemy ship they had sacrificed so much to defeat. As Stormfront sailed towards them, it took another half an hour until the flagship floundered and finally tipped to stern, its bow pointing skyward as the rear of the ship submerged for good.

She could see western troops, including a half-dozen Imbic jumping overboard like rats as they realised they weren't going to make it to land. Even so, it wasn't until Stormfront pulled up alongside them and lowered ropes that the behemoth gunship finally disappeared beneath the waves.

"Good riddance," Mick muttered as he preceded her up the ladder.

'The first duty of a mage is to Jeranon as a whole. On occasion, to that end, battles must be sacrificed so that wars may be won.'
Excerpt from 'The Gift.'

CHAPTER 19

DUTY

"You lost my ship," Wrigley said as she climbed to the deck of the Stormfront.

She looked at him as Millard climbed up behind her, but there was no malice in the words, only tiredness and pain.

"Captain Henely?" he asked, steeling himself for the answer he seemed to know was to come.

"Killed in the volley that tore off our stern," She replied in the same workmanlike tone.

Wrigley nodded stiffly. "A good man."

Johanna nodded her agreement. "What's next?"

Wrigley looked at her as though he were about to make some acid remark. Instead, he turned to look out into the darkness beyond the rail, studying the chaotic tangle of ships still engaged in the fight.

"Next, we get you and your people off this ship, to the shore, and on your way to Harverness."

Johanna strangely found herself wanting to protest. The fight wasn't done. The remaining western forces were still equal to their own. They still needed her.

And yet, wasn't this what she had wanted since the moment she'd woken on the island? A way to return home.

The time and people around her to recover her memories and her life. Why did his suggesting it make it seem dirty, tainted in some way she couldn't explain?

His gaze shifted back and then past her.

"Glad to see you alive Michael. Take the helm," he said.

"Aye sir," the man replied with a friendly nod to Johanna as he passed.

The Kingfisher's helmsman relieved the sailor stationed at the wheel, who looked glad to return to whatever it was he normally did. And just like that Michael was now the Stormfront's helmsman, and whatever she thought of Wrigley personally, he was also indisputably now its captain.

"This battle is a disaster," Wrigley said as he turned back towards the combined fleet's struggle.

Johanna walked over and joined him at the rail as they waited for the rest of the men to ascend from the lifeboat.

"Even taking out their flagship. Even with half the forces originally arrayed against us now at the bottom of the ocean, it's too close to call."

Johanna looked at him for a long moment. Wrigley's face was not one of defeat, but of icy determination.

"What are you going to do?" she asked, not sure she wanted to hear the answer.

He pursed his lips for a moment before speaking.

"I'm going to take command of the fleet. I'll take the few operational and unengaged ships we have left and start eliminating enemy vessels, beginning with those which have already made landfall."

"You are?" Johanna blurted out, shocked at the audacity of it. "There must be someone out there who ranks above X.O. still in the fight. You could end up court martialled."

Wrigley nodded. "You're almost certainly correct. But look around, this is chaos. There's no one in charge, no centralised plan. If any of the admiralty still lives, their ships are too engaged to do anything but defend themselves."

Johanna looked out at the tangle of ships vying for supremacy, fearing he was right.

"You'll need us if that's your plan," she said.

"Again, likely correct, Mage Johanna. However right now Jeranon needs you more. Someone in authority has to make it through the enemy lines on land and report. Whether or not we win here today, the northern fleet is to all intents and purposes no longer a viable military force. Not to mention the Bulwark Islands are no longer under Jeranonian control. Harverness lies less than a hundred leagues to the southwest and is the closest major city. It also houses the northern army, so you'll find help from Duke Gerara there if he's not already on the way."

Johanna was silent for a moment as she digested the implications of what he was saying.

"You don't think we can win, do you?"

Wrigley looked at her, taking her measure before pitching his voice so only they could hear.

"I don't know. Which is why I can't take the chance of you staying. If we lose, the countryside around this region will suffer greatly. If we lose and ten thousand more of their troops make landfall without the army being warned of our demise, it will be far, far worse. Besides, this isn't a free pass. Plenty of western troops have already made landfall. You may be in more danger if you go than if you stay. So I need to know, will you do this thing? Can you?" he said, motioning to her broken arm with his chin.

She grimaced. Standing saturated on the deck next to Wrigley with her arm in a sling, there was nothing imposing or authoritative about the way she looked. For an instant she flashed back to Trelmaine's ambush on the island, her hands raised in imitation of casting a spell. That probably wouldn't help right now. Still, it caused a slight smile to tug at the corner of her lips.

"I'll go," she said. "It needs to be done, and serves both our interests."

Wrigley nodded, and just like that it was decided.

"Sailors secure, Sir!" someone called from across the deck.

"Secure the boat and come about!" Wrigley called back. "Rendezvous with Ravager and take us into range of those beached western ships. This is our home, and I don't remember inviting them!"

A cheer went up from the men, but Wrigley hardly seemed to notice.

He was good at this, she realised. Most of these men weren't even from the Kingfisher's crew, and already they were taking orders like he'd been with them for years. Maybe he really could take hold of their fractured fleet and make something worthwhile of it. She would likely never see him again after they made landfall, and it was a comforting thought to hold on to.

The sailors in the rigging trimmed the sheets and Michael got them moving on course. Stormfront skimmed through the dark water towards where Ravager was still picking up survivors from their three other ships. By the time they pulled alongside, the Ravager's 'captain' came to the rail to report.

"It's been ten minutes since we picked up the last

survivor, Sir. I think we've got everyone who's coming."

Wrigley nodded so the other commander could see.

"Follow us to shore, we're going to let off some passengers and make sure the western troops can't sail home to report how badly they've hurt us."

The officer, whatever his rank had been this morning, saluted in acknowledgement, and Wrigley returned the gesture.

"Let's go," he said to Michael.

The two surviving ships were both damaged, but not critically. The Ravager had lost a mast, and Stormfront's port hull was damaged. But they could both still sail, both still fight.

"Have your men ready to disembark please. We'll be able to cover you, but our window for launching the boat will be small."

Johanna looked at him for a moment, wondering if she'd misjudged him at first after all.

"Thank you for everything," she said in a tone neutral enough that he could take it any way he desired.

"I wouldn't. By sunrise you may wish I'd left you on that island."

She didn't know how to respond to that, so nodded and walked back over to where Mick and Millard were waiting.

"We're going ashore and making for Harverness, gather up the men."

Mick grinned and left to carry out the order.

"He seems cheerful," Johanna remarked as the sodden man moved out of earshot.

"He gets seasick," Millard responded with a slight grin of his own.

"Ah."

"Why Harverness?" Millard added after a moment. "Surely Northwatch has alrea… Oh."

"Exactly. With the wave taking out the castle before the battle began, the duke may not even know the fleet is engaged. We just don't know. The entire northern army could be five miles from here, ready to crush the invaders, or just as likely still sleeping in their barracks several days' march away."

"We'll find them and report in, either way," Millard said.

Johanna nodded, feeling the cold now that she had a moment to stand still.

They were all wet, tired, and on edge from the stress of the battle, but their journey was far from over. A small knot of men appeared over the next few minutes, and Undu brought several canteens and a few small packs of supplies he'd requisitioned from the Stormfront's galley.

"We'll have to ration for a few days, but we'll make it on these supplies," the arborii quartermaster apologised as he handed them out.

"Thank you, Undu," Johanna said as she took a canteen and awkwardly secured it to her belt with one hand. She should have thought of that herself. What kind of leader marched without bringing food for her men?

The shore was fast approaching now, and a line of eight western ships were beached about a mile west of where the cliffs began.

Stormfront angled in towards them, then turned sharply to port, bringing its guns to bear and firing a volley into the first of the vessels. Ravager came in behind them and added to the damage, but Stormfront had already moved on, her gun crews reloading to fire on the next in line.

Wrigley ordered them to come to a stop near the last western vessel and nodded back at Johanna.

"Good luck. Lower the boat, continue firing!" he ordered his crew.

A pair of sailors rushed over to untie the knots that released the lifeboat, and it dropped to the water with a splash. One of the men threw the ladder over the side, and she watched it unroll as one end fell towards the boat.

Mick was the first to disembark, Johanna went next.

Climbing a rope ladder wasn't the easiest thing to do with one hand, and she slipped halfway. Mick caught her before she could either hit her head on the hard wood of the boat, or end up back in the ocean. He gave her a now familiar grin, but said nothing, for which she was grateful. The others made their way into the lifeboat a little more gracefully. As soon as they were all accounted for, Millard ordered them to take up the oars and begin rowing to shore.

All eight of them, she thought bitterly. Of Trelmaine's original crew only six remained. Millard, Mick, Colbar, three others whose names she didn't know, and at this point couldn't bring herself to ask. Plus herself and Undu. That was all.

The night air was chilling, and if nothing else she was looking forward to drying off in tomorrow's sun. As they rowed towards the rocky outcrop at the end of the beach, the Stormfront and Ravager continued pounding the beached western ships with cannon fire. The darkness was their ally now. The area inland would be crawling with western troops, and they would have to move quietly until they'd gained some distance. If they survived until sunrise without being spotted, they should be far enough away that they could make it to Harverness without the enemy catching up.

'Home is the place at the beginning of a journey.'
Arborii Proverb.

CHAPTER 20

THE LONG ROAD HOME

The lifeboat made a crunching noise as it ran up onto the rocky surface which was all the tsunami had left of the beach. Somewhere, on the ocean floor between the coast and the islands, the very earth had shifted enough to cause that massive ripple of destruction. She could only imagine what that upheaval might have looked like up close. She had no idea what time it was, but dawn couldn't be too far away.

Ahead of her, soldiers began jumping out of the boat, filing out the front end to stay relatively dry.

Mick waited back long enough to offer her a hand, but even with her broken arm she didn't need it. He shrugged and returned to scanning the tree line ahead.

The western troops were out there somewhere. The only bit of good news she could take from the situation was that they were trying to make their way inland, not defending this stretch of beach. With any luck, most or all of them had moved on.

For now the sky remained dark, the stars offering a dim light that let them see the unobstructed beach, but nothing at all beyond that first row of trees. There could be an army waiting for them, or no one at all.

Millard glanced around, and seeing them all safely on land motioned them to follow as he headed up the beach, skirting the rough cliff wall on their left. The bare rock was rough and free of dirt as every other surface scoured by the wave had been. The tall old trees ahead must have had deep roots to stay planted against that force.

A minute passed as they snuck up the beach, obscured by the darkness of the cliff. Johanna kept looking around, expecting to see a group of Augrahl, or worse yet, Imbic, charging at them from the tree line.

Millard turned back to them for a moment.

"So far so good," he said with a relieved grin as an arrow sprouted from his neck.

For a long moment Johanna's mind couldn't make sense of what her eyes were showing her. At least, not until the sergeant's eyes rolled up, and he crumpled, dead before he hit the ground.

"Archers!" Undu yelled as Mick bolted forward to drag Millard's body further into the shadow of the cliff. They were still looking around for the source of the shot when another man fell with a muffled scream. She saw him hit, and some distant part of her mind calculated the angle the arrow must have arced in on.

"The trees!" she shouted at the remaining men. "They're in the trees!"

A low whistling began, and some animal part of her understood it was caused by dozens, if not hundreds, of arrows arcing down from the sky.

She felt a surge of panic worse than anything since the lion had jumped onto the rock in front of her, and a bright blue wall of… something, appeared.

"Get behind me!" she screamed, part adrenalin, part

panic, and part fury that Millard was dead. Killed just for trying to walk up a beach.

The men scrambled in behind her as the arrows fell from the darkness with enough force to snap some of them as they hit the cliff behind.

A score of impacts hit her shield, but it held firm. She knew it could handle a lot of damage from her fight with the Imbic, but not an infinite amount.

She sent a delving spell into Millard's body just in case, but both his and the other soldiers' story had ended here. They couldn't even stop to give them a proper burial. They had to get off this beach.

A second volley of arrows hummed through the air. This time no one was hit though, and Johanna motioned them to stay with her as she began moving up the beach again. Mick lagged for a moment with Millard's body, and for an instant she wasn't sure the dour man was going to follow at all. A guttural scream from the tree line got his attention. As the first western troops sprinted towards them he unsheathed Millard's sword from its scabbard and started walking.

She thought he was getting back into cover of her shield at last, but he didn't even glance her way as he continued straight on towards the charging western troops.

Before he could make it a dozen spans, the tree line exploded in a litany of detonations. Several of the huge trunks were felled, and dirt and branches were spraying in every direction.

"What?" Undu shouted. "Was that you?"

Johanna shook her head as the tree line was rocked again, several more trees falling amongst themselves and firing splinter sized projectiles all around the area.

The charging western troops looked back, hesitating as they realised their reinforcements were no longer coming. There were about a dozen Nostahl, a pair of the larger Augrahl warriors, and in the back, a horrifying creature that almost had to be an Imbic.

This one's mutations were extreme. Its flesh was the pinky-white of half-cooked chicken, and it was running along the ground on at least thirty legs like a squat, spherical centipede. Five long arms extended from the main mass at random intervals, and each carried an enormous blade of varying description, each as different as the arm that wielded it. If it had a head, she couldn't see where it was through the glow of her shield.

A third volley of cannon fire rocked the tree line, and Johanna's mind finally caught up to the fact that Captain Wrigley must have seen they were in trouble when she raised the shield. He was doing what he could to cover their escape.

No more arrows were incoming, and Undu and the other four men drew their weapons and moved out of cover to catch up to Mick.

Without breaking stride, the man cut down the two first Nostahl to reach him with savage blows far harder than he needed to break the diminutive creatures' guard. He wasn't taking Millard's death well. The others ran to join him as he spun and cut another charging Nostahl nearly in half. He kept walking and blocked a blow from the next opponent before stabbing it so hard in an underhand blow with Millard's sword that he lifted the creature clear off the ground.

The others arrived as the first of the Augrahl reached them and then the rest of the Nostahl. One of the soldiers went down as a half-dozen of the vicious little creatures chose him as their target. Undu tried to keep the second Augrahl from joining the melee by intercepting it directly.

None of that was her problem. The Imbic was coming fast, scuttling across the rocky beach as it bore down on her. She could hear the rapid slapping of its bare feet on the rock, and a part of her mind recoiled. A small part. As the disgusting thing charged, she imagined it on fire, and with a now familiar click in her mind, so it was.

The Imbic screeched in a tone no human voice had ever uttered. It didn't stop as it ploughed into her shield, beating at it with the weapons in all five of its arms.

It must have thought that killing her would halt the spell. It was wrong. She wasn't maintaining it, and had already moved on. Millard's sudden death had left her cold and numb, and as the creature hammered at her shield, she ignored it. The second Augrahl had Undu on the ground and she turned towards them, imagining a rope of air strangling the grey-skinned creature.

Click.

The Augrahl didn't seem to understand what was happening for a moment, then looked up in panic as Undu broke free and ran the westerner through with his blade. She let the spell go.

Mick had dispatched the other Augrahl already, and seeing their more powerful allies' fate, the remaining Nostahl were attempting to flee.

"Burn," she decreed.

Click.

All five of the diminutive figures howled as they burst into flames hot enough to turn them to ash before they could even fall.

The Imbic was down now, most of the flames quenched, but still somehow alive.

Mick walked over and stabbed it through the main mass. It made a sound, but barely moved. Mick struck it again, and again, and again as she watched, the violence of his reaction not evoking an emotional response in her the way she thought it should.

"Enough!" Undu commanded.

The sound of his voice in the otherwise still night was enough to make Mick hesitate, look back at the arborii soldier, then back to the Imbic lying dead before him. He lowered his sword and gave it one last kick for good measure before walking away.

Johanna watched him go. She should have stopped him sooner. She knew it, but all she could think of was Millard's body cooling a few dozen spans away, and the pointless fate he'd met at these creatures' hands.

Why did the westerners hate them so? Why had they come here, invading Jeranon yet again? They'd brought enough troops and firepower to cripple the northern fleet, but nowhere near enough to launch a full-scale invasion with any real chance of success. What was the point?

Since waking on the island, she had stumbled from one violent encounter to another. Her lion seemed almost gentle at this point. She had to get back home, had to warn the army and report back to the Archmagi at Harverness. She needed to get her memories back to make sense of everything which had happened over the last half a phase.

None of that could happen here.

She walked away from the butchered Imbic, wondering why she felt so little for it.

It wasn't until she turned away that it hit her like a slap

in the face. Three more of her men were down, and Colbar had a nasty gash across his cheek that needed attention. She hurried over and placed her good hand over the wound, working the Gift whilst Undu confirmed the fate of the soldier who had fallen to the Nostahl.

He shook his furry head when she glanced his way, but his overly large eyes told her all she needed to know. Only five of them remained.

"Let's go," she said as soon as Colbar's face was mended.

Mick stood from Millard's fallen side without hesitation this time, sheathing his own sword and keeping Millard's in hand as he moved to the front of the group. Undu took up a place beside her, and Colbar and the other man brought up the rear.

She really needed to ask his name.

A final round of cannon fire smashed into the tree line as they reached the top of the beach. Soon enough they arrived at the place where the cliff top was met by the incline of beach they were on. Off to their left the watchtower was under siege by dozens of enemy troops, to the right, the tree line was a study in devastation. Bent and broken branches and trunks lay every which way. Between the two, a small gap existed in front of them filled only with darkness. If they could make it to the shadowed area unseen, they might sneak past whatever western troops remained, and break through to safer lands beyond.

The sun was perhaps an hour away. They needed to be gone before then.

Mick motioned to the darkness before them, and she nodded. What choice did they have?

Mick bent low and ducked out from the last piece of cover. They all crept behind, hoping desperately that none of the westerner's noticed their passing. It would only take one.

By the time they reached the darkness, Johanna's heart was racing so hard she had to stop for a moment to recover. Her broken arm was aching from the extended run, but there was no sign they'd been spotted. Mick motioned for them to keep moving. They had to get out in front of the enemy, otherwise they would be risking capture or death all the way back to Harverness.

The trees grew thicker and the night impossibly dark as they headed south under the thin canopy.

Mick grunted, and they were forced to stop as the big man extracted himself from a thorny bush.

"We can't move forward in this," he whispered in frustration.

"We'll rest until the sun comes up and leave as soon as we can make out the ground in front of us. It shouldn't be long," she agreed.

The others stood around for a moment as if unsure what to do until Undu sat down, facing back towards the beach to keep a watch. The arborii's movement acted as a signal for the rest of them, and even Johanna found herself drawn to the ground, exhausted both physically and emotionally. In the distance, they could hear the tower siege continuing. She doubted whoever was in there could win that fight, but perhaps they could resist long enough for the fleet to gain supremacy and come to their aid.

She wanted to believe she wasn't leaving them to their deaths. It was a thin hope, but one she would take. She had to.

Sometime later, she realised she could see her few remaining men a little clearer. She stood, and the movement gained the attention of the others.

"It's time."

There were determined and exhausted nods all round, and Undu's tail swished impatiently like a cat.

Mick moved forward without a word, taking the lead yet again. It was the most dangerous position, but she doubted she could talk him out of it even had she been inclined. He was clearly set on protecting the last few of them left, and she wasn't about to take that thin sliver of purpose away from him.

The going was hard, and Mick had to use Millard's sword several times to cut away vines and thick, ropy bushes which blocked their way. The light was getting better by the minute though, and soon they were making good time.

Sounds of battle had faded behind them now, and they fell into a rhythm of taking turns cutting away the underbrush so they could progress. Undu had taken to the trees and was watching their back for signs of pursuit, but so far hadn't sounded an alert. It was back-breaking work, but sometime after midday they cut their way through a tangle of vines to reveal a grassed valley with little cover for miles ahead.

"What do you think?" she asked as Mick came up beside her.

He scowled. "Perfect place for an ambush if they got here ahead of us."

Johanna nodded. As soon as they left the trees, they would be visible to anyone for miles around who cared to look this way.

"Short of going a week out of our way, we're out of options," he said.

Mick sighed, waves of weariness radiating off him in an almost visible display. "The army needs to know what's coming their way. So I'm going first. If they come for me, get back into the forest and stay hidden. Head west for a day and try again. If I'm still clear after a mile, join me."

"You don't have to do this," she said, her voice choking up. "It doesn't have to be you."

He looked at her strangely for a moment and bent down to snatch something off the ground.

"Remember that time I threw a rock at your head because I didn't trust you?"

Johanna couldn't decide whether to scowl or smile, like it had become some kind of private joke between them. So why did she feel as though she wanted to cry?

He reached out and took her good hand, placing a palm sized rock in it.

She looked at it for a long moment before she understood his meaning, and this time couldn't stop a small grin.

"If you truly feel the need…"

She looked him in the eye and was about to drop the stone back to earth. She did trust him. More than she'd realised until now apparently, and his gesture deserved more than that.

She placed the stone in a small pocket on her sleeve and buttoned it up before raising an eyebrow.

"Not this time, Private. But I'll be sure to keep it handy for a future date."

Mick just stared at her. Then couldn't help himself from

laughing loudly enough that he had to stop himself again or risk giving away their location.

"Sure, why not?" he said, and walked out into the grassland with Millard's sword in hand as though he had not a care in the world.

For tense moments they watched as he walked farther and farther away from the safety of the trees. One minute passed, and Undu caught up with them. Two. Three minutes, and Mick kept walking. If there was going to be an attack, the westerners would wait until he was far from the trees. That way they could be sure to intercept him before he could return to the relative safety of the forest. If it was going to happen at all, it would be soon.

Mick continued walking.

Johanna screamed as something cold and hard bit deep into the flesh of her back. She fell forward with a gasp and as she twisted, saw the grey skin and sharpened teeth of the Nostahl which had snuck up behind her. The creature was grinning as it examined the six- inch-long blade covered in blood it was holding. Her blood.

Colbar struck off its head before it could manage a second blow, but a rustling in the bush announced they were no longer alone.

"Get her out of here!" Colbar ordered Undu, and the Arborii soldier didn't hesitate.

He wrapped an arm under her good one and hoisted her up none too gently from where she had fallen.

The first step was agony, the second worse, and her leg was already slick with blood.

That was bad, some distant part of her mind informed her as Undu took most of her weight and guided her into the open fields.

She could hear steel meeting steel behind her, but couldn't turn enough to see if Colbar needed help. They hadn't gone fifty spans when the sounds stopped with a muffled yell.

Undu glanced back and then stopped. He lowered her to the ground as gently as he could and faced back the other way, drawing his sword from its sheath.

She turned back towards the forest, though it felt as if she were tearing the wound as she did so, and gasped at what she saw.

A half-dozen Augrahl led a score of the smaller Nostahl out from the tree line. Colbar and the soldier whose name she'd meant to ask had never had a chance. At least there were no more Imbic.

The grey-skinned brute in the lead waved at them with his sword, and the Nostahl charged. The Augrahl themselves stood back and watched in what she could have sworn was amusement. With their two-foot-long black horns and rows of sharpened teeth, it was difficult to tell.

Undu moved to block them.

"No. Stand aside, I need a clear line of sight," she said before he could block her view.

Undu did as he was told, and she began thinking about the grass around her being on fire.

Click.

For a hundred spans in every direction the grass blazed to an inferno for half a second before it was consumed.

That was not what she'd intended.

She'd wanted a slow burn with lots of smoke to camouflage their retreat. Instead the fuel was incinerated in an instant, burning and scarring the legs of Nostahl and

Augrahl alike, but not doing enough damage to kill them.

Half of them collapsed in pain, but more struggled on. Too many. The Augrahl made a guttural howling, and five of them charged along with the Nostahl. One fell almost immediately, but they were made of sterner stuff than their smaller compatriots. Or perhaps they just had better armour. Either way, they weren't nearly as incapacitated as she might have hoped.

"Any other ideas?" Undu asked nervously as the first of the Nostahl grew close.

"Not good ones," she replied as she glanced behind her. Mick was coming fast, but was still at least a hundred and fifty spans off. At this rate he would get to them just in time to see her die.

Undu jabbed at the charging Nostahl. As his thrust hit the mark, he stepped deftly aside to remain unencumbered as the creature fell.

There were too many more just a step behind.

Too close, she thought. She had to space them out so that Undu wouldn't be immediately overwhelmed.

She reached out her good hand as the idea hit her. Her back screamed in protest where the Nostahl had stabbed her, but she was focused on other things.

She imagined the spell she'd propelled the Kingfisher's broken hull with.

Click.

A gust of wind tore from her fingers and knocked a Nostahl back a full fifty spans. She watched it, as did the Augrahl who were following close behind. The Nostahl ahead of it continued to charge and Undu was about to be swamped.

She repeated the spell, aiming for the knot of troops and

shoving three of them over thirty spans through the air. They didn't get up either.

Undu sliced and blocked as four more Nostahl reached him, even jumping at one point as one of them tried to take out his legs.

They were too close. If she used the same spell now she could kill the arborii soldier by mistake. But what else could she do? The Augrahl had spread out now so her spells couldn't catch them in a group. The lead creature reared its head back and uttered an inhuman bellow before they all charged together. Right at her.

She hit the leader with the air spell. Undu would have to prevail without her. The Augrahl fell over and tumbled a few spans, but wasn't seriously hurt. Why hadn't that worked? The Augrahl were certainly heavier, but not enough to make the difference between throwing one fifty spans or five. The others didn't break stride.

She needed something more, and she needed it right now. She frantically searched her memories for the most violent thing she might be capable of.

The Imbic.

The first one, when Trelmaine had been killed. It had wanted to eat her, and she had made it explode somehow. There was a cry from her rear and Undu went down, the three remaining Nostahl jumping on him without hesitation, cutting and stabbing with glee.

She felt a fury rise in her like nothing she could remember, and focused all her will on duplicating whatever she had done to that first Imbic mutation. She didn't know what it was, but she could still see its open maw, see it lowering her towards its rows of sharpened teeth, see it explode into its constituent parts without warning. The memory was visceral. She focused her imagination on making it happen again.

Click.

Everything around her for fifty spans erupted in a fountain of gore. Even the trees at the edge of the forest shattered into splinters in an instant. It was though reality itself had come apart.

She stood there in shock as the viscera of a score of enemy, but intelligent beings, fountained out and slapped to the ground. It was a sound she knew she would remember to the end of her days.

Shaking, she looked back to see if Undu had survived the Nostahl assault, and collapsed to her knees when the only sign she found of him was a small patch of torn blue fur some distance away.

"No..." she whispered as the realisation of what she'd just done hit her squarely in the face.

She'd feared this all along. What she'd warned Trelmaine about before that first disastrous ambush. She had never regained full control of her powers since waking on the other island, and now she'd killed a good man, arborii, whatever, along with the enemy.

It was a less painful death than the Nostahl would have given him, some distant part of her mind informed her. She stamped it down hard, and then Mick was there, putting an arm around her shoulder and lifting her to her feet.

"We have to go! There's no telling how many more are coming this way."

All she could do was stare at the spot where Undu had been fighting for his life. For their lives. The spot where she'd betrayed and murdered him.

"For what it's worth," Mick said as he shifted his grip

and picked her up as though she were a child. "I doubt he was still alive, and if he was, he probably would have thanked you for ending what they were doing to him by then."

He was already walking back to the forest edge by the time he finished talking. His words registered, but were so far from anything she could process right now that she didn't feel the need to react. She didn't feel anything other than the pain. She shifted somewhat in his grip so the wound in her back didn't hurt as much. Doing so jostled her arm and sent a spike of pain up it. A small reminder that her life had consisted of more than just this one terrible moment.

"Put me down," she said.

"No. Sorry, Mage Johanna, but we need to move faster than you can walk right now. And you wouldn't get far with that wound anyway. Once we're clear, I'll rig up a stretcher so you can recover as we travel."

She wanted to argue, but as inappropriate as it was, what she wanted even more was to sleep and let someone else take responsibility for a while. She fought the urge as long as she could, but before they had even reached what Mick considered a safe distance, she felt herself becoming more and more exhausted. Maybe it was the blood loss, or maybe she was going into shock.

Or maybe I just feel safe for the first time I can remember, she thought as her head slumped against his shoulder and she fell into a deep sleep.

The next thing she knew she was being jostled, but not by Mick. A strap across her chest loosely restrained her, and her legs were bumping along uneven ground.

"What?" She got out of a parched throat.

The movement stopped, and someone lowered her gently to the ground. Her back stung as it made contact, but not as much as she thought it should have.

"Glad to see you're awake," Mick's voice said with a smile as he came around and into her line of sight. "It was touch and go there for a while."

She tried to sit up, but it was too much for her back. The wound felt strange, and she felt around behind her with her good arm. It was packed with bandages and sewn up in a serviceable fashion that would keep her alive, but definitely leave a scar.

"Where did you find a needle and thread?" She croaked, and followed it up with, "And how long has it been?"

"Four days," he said without hesitation. "And as for the supplies, I'm a ranger. I always keep enough basic materials on me in the field to dress at least one wound."

"Water?" he inquired.

Johanna nodded, suddenly parched. She went to drink deeply from the canteen he offered but then stopped.

"How much do we have?" she asked.

Mick grinned. "There're streams all around here, you can take your fill. Nice of you to ask this time though."

Johanna put the canteen to her lips and drunk it dry. When she was finished, she looked at him with all the amusement her abused body would allow her.

"Just didn't feel like getting hit by another rock."

Mick laughed. "Yeah, sorry about that. In my defence, I really expected you would stop it if you were who you said you were."

"I know," she replied. "I heard you telling Trelmaine before you realised I was awake."

"Ah. That explains a lot."

"How so," she asked as he handed her a cloth full of strawberries.

"Came across them yesterday," he said by way of explanation. "Figured you'd be hungry, and I couldn't risk lighting a fire. Oh and in answer to your question, most magi wouldn't take a blow to their pride half as well. If it's not too much to say, your lot can be a mite arrogant. Probably comes from being able to have whatever they can imagine. You seem more or less okay though," he added with another grin.

"Thanks so much," she said, not sure whether it was an insult or a compliment.

"So where are we?" she asked once she'd finished the fruit.

The corner of Mick's mouth twitched, and he stood and looked around. The trees here were sparse and thin trunked, with high foliage that didn't obstruct their line of sight much.

"As best I can make out, we're less than a hundred miles from the city…"

"But?" She prompted when he failed to say anything more.

His brows drew together. "I don't know. Something's off. We should be seeing people coming and going by now, even if only a few. But there's nothing."

"Is that a problem?"

"Not unless it becomes one," he replied. "Anyway, get some more rest. In a day or two you might be able to walk again, but for now we'll make better time if you stay in the stretcher."

Without waiting for an answer, he moved behind her and lifted the stretcher back into a diagonal position and began dragging her across Jeranon again like a bag of gear.

It wasn't dignified. It wasn't comfortable. As the motion of his gait rocked the stretcher back and forth, she found the food in her belly and water that she'd drunk conspired to make her sleepy again. She let herself relax. Right now there wasn't much else she could do.

A tremor in the ground woke her sometime later, though it was hard to say if it was the same day or not.

She felt the tremor again. "What?"

"Shhh… Stay here and stay quiet." Mick said, his tone leaving no room for argument. "Something's coming."

She struggled to sit up, undoing the knot in the strip of fabric that was holding her to the stretcher with her one good hand. Her back protested, stiff and sore, but she made it, and peeked over the rock Mick had stashed her behind. Nothing was there. The ground trembled again, and Mick drew Millard's sword as well. The veteran ranger was on high alert, scanning the woods around them for any sign of movement.

Different woods, her mind supplied. The foliage here was far denser, and a deeper green in general. Her line of sight was less than twenty spans in any direction. The ground rumbled again, closer this time. Whatever was coming, it wasn't a natural occurrence like the aftershocks of the tsunami. Something was shaking the ground itself, and the primitive part of her brain was screaming at her to run, to be anywhere but here.

In the distance, a tree toppled to the ground with a crash, then another. Mick glanced at her, and even from here she could see the worry in his eyes.

He came back over and helped her to her feet.

"We need to go. Can you walk?"

Johanna just nodded, unwilling even to whisper as another tree fell less than a hundred spans away.

It made her back ache like nothing she'd ever felt, but Mick sheathed one of the swords and supported her weight on that side. Together they moved away from the disturbance as quietly as they knew how.

The ground was rumbling now. Not the occasional tremor, but a sustained vibration that was increasing by the second. A tree fell not fifty spans behind them, and Mick glanced back, his eyes going wide.

"Run!" he commanded as he tried to pull her along with him.

She did her best to keep up, but her back was in agony and her broken arm was being jostled, adding to the pain.

"What is it?" She gasped, already at the edge of her strength.

"Underground," he puffed back. "And gaining."

She tried to twist around to see what it was, but all she could see was an eight-foot-wide line where the soil was being churned and uprooted. Something below was moving through it like a worm.

"Stop! We can't outrun it!" she shouted as the disturbance thundered towards them, knocking down another tree as it advanced.

Mick halted regretfully, and they spun to face whatever was coming.

"We were so close," he muttered as he once again drew the second sword and moved away, motioning her to do the same. Whatever it was, it seemed there was only one.

She limped out of its direct line of movement, motioning Mick to go the other direction, and hoping against hope it didn't know they were there.

For an instant it seemed hesitant, confused, and in that moment she knew they were in trouble. If it hadn't known they were there, it would have continued on despite their separation.

The disturbance surged into motion again, heading directly for Mick, who dived out of the way at the last instant. The wild leap saved his life as a vast mouth, at least six feet in diameter rose out of the ground, the maw full of shark-like teeth. Its half-cooked-chicken looking flesh proclaimed it only one thing.

"Die!" she screamed at the bizarre Imbic mutation as she set it on fire.

The thing rolled violently in the dirt, dousing the flames, and knocking a tree over with its tail as it thrashed around, exposing the rest of its body.

It was twenty feet or more long, a cylinder with hundreds of protrusions along every part of its flanks. The creature seemed to use them to move somehow, and it horrified her that some had hands or feet on their ends, a few even sported screaming and distorted faces. How had this race of monsters ever come to exist?

A fleshy compartment on its front opened to reveal a single massive eye. She shuddered, despite being the size of a large blue melon, it appeared completely human. It even blinked.

Mick thrust his swords into the creature, and it spun, hitting him with its tail end and knocking him back a dozen paces.

It turned towards her, the eye seeming to take her measure. It opened its maw wide and charged. Johanna felt her shield go up as the creature bit down, thousands of teeth raking the light blue sphere as it charged on, expecting her to be chewed up. In instants she was out the other side, the shield holding on by a thread. This must be how it moved through the dirt with such speed, grabbing the substrate both from the inside and out.

She set it burning again now that the whole thing was visible. She didn't dare make it explode for fear of killing Mick as well.

The creature rolled again and doused the flames in an instant. What else could she do? It was too massive for the air spell to jolt it away. She was running out of options. Mick was up now and had the creature's attention. It charged, and she used a gust of air on Mick instead, throwing him aside as it tried to eat him the same way it had with her.

The creature turned towards her, seeming to understand what had happened. Despite its massive mutations, could this… thing, be as intelligent as her or Mick? It was a disturbing thought.

The creature charged her again. Instead of engulfing her with its maw this time, it changed direction at the last instant and whipped its tail around. The Imbic struck her shield like a hammer, the force of the blow flinging her through the air like a toy. She hit a tree, hard. It wasn't till she landed that she saw her shield had gone out and a piece of branch was embedded in her side. She pulled it out. The wound was deep, and had left a large gash across her right-side above her hip.

How much blood did one have to lose before it became life-threatening?

The last thing she thought as the world faded to an agonised black was that it didn't matter. She had to get up. She had to help Mick.

'We control all elements of the world except our own fate. Why should we not rule you? Despite our slight numbers, our power far exceeds your own, as does our ambition.'
Excerpt from a fifteen-hundred-year-old document detailing the trial of Eldrik the Black.

CHAPTER 21

THE PATH OF PRIDE

Today was the day.

Everything was in place. The people who mattered had arrived. Nothing remained but to show them all what she had done. What she had created. A thousand years from now they would talk about this day as the start of a new era. A thousand years from now, they would still speak her name.

"They're waiting for you," Archmage Joram said from beside her.

She looked up, her thoughts interrupted, and nodded. She hadn't heard him approach.

"You're sure everything is in place?" he asked.

"It better be," Johanna replied. "I won't get a second shot at this."

Joram nodded. "Good. If this works, I intend to leverage your success by having the king name us as the third legitimate branch of the College of the Arts. We've been the equal of Miralthrall for decades. It's time our place here was written into law."

She nodded back. She didn't care what he did on a political level. Her ambitions lay elsewhere.

"I still can't believe he came. You know he's out there, right? First time he's left the capital in six years. King Erich has travelled a long way for this, so don't let him down. Or me," Joram told her in an offhand manner, which belied the archmage's nervousness. He was normally more subtle than that.

"I wouldn't have invited him if I wasn't sure it would work," she said, partly in an attempt to reassure her old teacher, and partly to make him go away. She had more important things to do right now than handhold the man who wanted to be the first head of a new branch of the College of the Arts.

"Joram. Go take your seat, I'll begin in a moment."

He nodded nervously. "All right. Good luck," he said, then turned and left.

She took a deep breath once he was out of sight, clearing her head. It would all work fine. She was ready.

She walked along the short length of corridor, paused in front of a door for an instant, and pushed it open with the Gift. She strode into the octant like she owned it, and it wasn't far from the truth. The small octagonal arena had been built to her specifications, and in the coming years, the area would serve as a waystation for those arriving and departing.

As she entered, the background noise of multiple conversations ended, leaving her footsteps loud and oddly distracting as she approached the podium at the octant's centre. In front of her, behind a wrought iron divider, several rows of stands had been placed, and were full to brimming with some of the most powerful magi in Jeranon.

Once she was ready at the podium, the doors at the rear of the stands opened, and the assembled magi and archmagi stood. Joram led King Erich inside, flanked by a pair of royal guards even here. They strode to the seats reserved for them at the front of the stands, directly in line with her, and took their places, the guards remaining at their backs. Once the two men were seated, the rest of the occupants returned to their places. Now it was all on her.

"Your Majesty, esteemed archmagi and magi, thank you for coming today, especially those of you who have travelled from across Jeranon to be here. Hopefully we can get you home a little quicker."

There were a few small laughs from the crowd, but she had only wanted to break the ice, not become a comedy act, so she moved on.

"As you are all here, you already know what I am about to attempt, the translocation of a living being from one place to another via the Gift." There was a stirring in the stands, and she had the distinct feeling that some of them had been under the mistaken impression that she had been joking about the subject of today's presentation.

"Make no mistake, I have already succeeded in this endeavour. Today I have called you here not to witness an experiment, but to make my findings public."

That set the crowd buzzing.

She left the podium to approach a small, stone pedestal. It was made of sandstone, about waist height, and octagonal to suit the mood of the day, though all that was irrelevant. The stand served only to draw the attention of the crowd. It was one of two equally spaced across the octant. Once she reached it, she took a handful of smooth river rocks from a pocket and laid them on its top before returning to the podium.

"Several years ago, I discovered the ability to make things disappear. Not to destroy them, but to remove them from existence. It took me a long time to understand this new ability, and longer to control it, but eventually…"

She waved her hand at the rocks to draw their attention, and the stones shimmered, disappearing, only to reappear a moment later on the second, empty pedestal. Someone gasped, and she tried to hide a grin. It was the least of what she would show them today.

"As you can see, translocation is not only possible, but has already been achieved. My next challenge was to send through something living. I started with plants, then insects, and finally mammals. The only time they did not complete their transits was when the spell was interrupted. Of a series run of five thousand living transits, only three failed, all of them variants of the common rose bush. I recommend further research to ascertain if this species is resistant to the translocation spell, or if the failures were a coincidental outlier."

She took a breath, looked to the side, and nodded to a servant waiting in the wings.

The man led a golden retriever out into the octant, bringing the freshly groomed dog to a halt near the pedestal, and ordering her to sit.

The dog obeyed, with what could only be described as a smile on its face, and the servant left.

Johanna concentrated on it for a moment, and the dog shimmered out of existence. It reappeared by the pile of rocks on the other side of the octant, happily panting away.

The retriever looked confused for a minute, but was otherwise unharmed.

She smiled and nodded to the crowd, and after a moment of stunned silence they roared to life, standing as one and applauding her achievement. The king raised an eyebrow, and her mentor, Joram, smiled as well.

She held up her hands to let them know she wasn't yet done, and they sat, eager for the next phase of the demonstration.

"If that was all I could achieve, it would change our commerce forever. Goods could be translocated from one city to another without shipping times and costs, or fear of piracy. Aid and relief could be sent to battlefields when the western nations strike, as they always do. No one in Jeranon would ever again go hungry due to natural disaster or crop failure, as we could resupply them within hours of knowing they needed help."

Joram nodded to her to continue. Only he knew what her full demonstration entailed. Or at least he thought he did. There were things even he didn't know she'd been working on. He wouldn't have allowed her to continue otherwise. He was always talking about how powerful the magi were, and how easily they could take Jeranon for themselves if they wanted. About how they had to be cautious of going further than the Giftless would allow, or their pride would lead to conflict. While she had no desire to seize power, she also had no interest in holding the magi back from becoming even more dangerous to their foes. It was a point they'd fundamentally disagreed on over the years. Joram had always argued that if they kept improving their knowledge of battle magic indefinitely, a time would come when the Giftless saw the magi themselves as the greatest threat.

And so Joram only knew about the first half of her research. Once the king understood its potential, it wouldn't matter whether her mentor approved or not.

Keeping the secret had been relatively easy. She had her own research space, as did all magi who wished to. Besides, already being engaged in College approved, long-term experiments, had meant no one was looking too closely at what she was doing with her time on a day-to-day basis.

She nodded to the servant again, who whistled to call back the dog.

The retriever dashed to her handler and a young man in the white-lined cloak of an apprentice mage entered the octant. With him, he carried a foot-wide metal cube which he placed on the nearest pedestal.

"This is Hue, an apprentice of the College and my assistant for the last two years," she introduced the young man to the assembled crowd.

"Your Majesty," he acknowledged in greeting.

"You see, it's not just property or lower life forms which can be translocated," she said without preamble.

Hue shimmered for a second and was gone, appearing at the other pedestal in less than a second. He blinked as his mind reoriented itself, and then waved to the crowd like he'd done a particularly difficult circus trick.

"Mage Johanna!" Joram interrupted as he stood, red faced and livid. "The College has not approved you for human trials. What are you doing?"

She had been hoping Joram wouldn't make a scene in public, but she couldn't allow him to derail her presentation. Even if it meant alienating the man who had taught her for most of her life. Instead of answering, she turned to face the king.

"I presume His Majesty wants to see how his armies will, from this day forward, be able to move from one battlefield to the next in a matter of moments?"

Joram's mouth opened and closed in deep fury as the king raised an eyebrow and contemplated the prospect.

"Continue, Mage Johanna," he commanded.

Joram sat again, his venomous gaze upon her. She would pay for both circumventing and then humiliating him later, of that she was certain. Once her demonstration was complete, however, even an archmage as powerful as he wouldn't be able to do much to her.

"Archmage Joram is correct in his assertion, Your Majesty, and I apologise for my subterfuge. However, the results of this research are too important to wait years, or even as much as a decade, for formal approval. The spell works. Now. Three phases ago I sent you an invitation to attend this unveiling, along with an item. Might I have your indulgence in telling the rest of those here today what that item was?"

King Erich looked both offput, and vaguely amused, but did as she had asked. He turned in his chair.

"It was a piece of paper on which Mage Johanna had requested I place the royal seal and the date I received it. Furthermore, she requested that I then pass this item to Archmage Inij, leader of the Aramarian College, for use during this very demonstration."

"Was my request granted, Your Majesty?" she asked, desperately hoping the answer was yes. If he hadn't done this small thing, her next demonstration would lack definitive proof, but it wouldn't be a total loss.

"I have known Archmage Inij since I was a child, and he seemed intrigued. Therefore I chose to grant your request."

"Thank you, Your Majesty," she said with profound relief. "I have contacted the archmage, and furthermore sent him a piece of arcana, a duplicate of the one you see here. Once charged, it will grant him the ability to cast this same spell from his end without needing to know the details."

There was another murmur from the crowd, one which caused her to smile.

"That's right, I can produce items of arcana to facilitate the translocation spell."

It was as large a breakthrough as the spell itself. If items of arcana could cast the translocation spell, even the weakest mage could eventually power them up and use them.

"I will now send Hue to Aramar. I expect the round trip to take no more than a minute."

The crowd was silent now, and she looked over at Hue. The man was ready. Nervous, but ready.

She closed her eyes, picturing the octant in Aramar in perfect detail. It was identical to this one in every respect, but for a stripe of colour on the far wall to help the casting mage identify to which octant the traveller was to be sent.

She opened her eyes and Hue vanished. Someone in the crowd gasped as though they hadn't believed she would actually go through with it.

"Right now Hue is reorienting himself in Aramar and conferring with Archmage Inij," she announced. It was a guess, but one that kept the crowd's attention occupied for the intervening seconds until he returned. She couldn't let their nervousness and excitement pull her off course. Joram was still glaring at her. If anything went wrong, or if apprentice Hue didn't return safely, she would no doubt bear the full force of his wrath.

"By now, Archmage Inij is powering the cube on his end, and we should see Hue again any second."

There was a pause, and nothing happened. She could feel the nervous energy coming off the crowd now, and even King Erich was leaning forward in his chair.

Another twenty seconds went by. What was taking so long? Inij was more than powerful enough to charge the cube by now. Had she made some terrible mistake? Had Hue ended up somewhere he wasn't supposed to, or worse, come to harm?

"Mage Johanna," Joram said in anger. "Where is my…"

Hue appeared out of nowhere, a vague, momentary shimmer like a heat haze the only sign he hadn't been standing there all along.

The young man blinked a few times as the crowd went silent again, then located her and nodded.

"You have it?" she asked. He smiled.

"Apprentice Hue, please give King Erich the item I sent you to recover from Aramar."

Hue strode over to the reigning monarch of Jeranon and handed him a small piece of paper. Johanna gave him a moment to look it over, eventually shaking his head in disbelief.

"Your Majesty, might I prevail upon you to show those assembled what you were just given.

The king nodded and stood. He held up the paper imprinted with the royal seal.

"This is the paper I signed phases ago, which I left with Archmage Inij in Aramar when I journeyed here. His signature and date appear below my own, and are today's."

The king sat again before addressing her.

"Mage Johanna, you have outdone yourself. You have my sincerest thanks on behalf of a grateful nation for the strides you have made here today."

Johanna felt herself blushing. All her years of work were about to pay off. Once she made the final demonstration of her presentation, they would immortalise her name among the greatest magi who ever lived.

"Thank you for your kind words, Your Majesty, but I have one thing left to show you."

"There's more!" Joram exclaimed, almost choking on the words.

The king gave him a sideways glance, but motioned for her to continue.

Johanna smiled. It was time.

"The primary focus of my research this last decade has been the translocation spell. I quickly realised, however, that the number of magi needed to operate the octants would become untenable once the arcana became more widespread. Therefore, I was faced with two theoretical solutions, neither of which was possible at the time. One. I could spend the next decade building thousands of these cubes, which could be used and recharged ad nauseam, and distributed to every octant we build. But they would quickly become impossible to track, breaking every law we have on maintaining strict controls over arcana, so they don't become a danger to the general population. Or two, I could make each cube do more. Since I have no desire to spend the next several years churning out these cubes, that only left me one viable avenue of research."

There were a few guffaws in the crowd. For most magi, constructing arcane items en masse was like doing paperwork for the Giftless. Boring and repetitive.

"For thousands of years, we magi have been restricted to casting spells on our own. We have been unable to link our powers due to the subtle differences between the intent and imagination of each individual involved. This discrepancy has always caused our shared spells to falter, no matter how accurately envisioned. The problem, at its core, is that each individual sees the world in a subtly different way. I have now overcome that deficiency."

They were staring at her now in silence, some aghast, some in awe, some as though she were lying through her teeth. Joram sat back in his chair, eyes wide, face pale, and definitely afraid of her. For the first time he seemed to realise that all their discussions of the magi's overwhelming power over the Giftless hadn't been idle speculation all these years.

"While the possibilities of this new frontier will not be fully explored for decades to come, for now, the cubes allow multiple magi to charge them at once. We've had the ability to make higher capacity, power-consuming arcana for years, but without an individual powerful enough to fill them, that extra capacity was pointless. These cubes overcome that failing of only allowing a single input, so long as the participating magi make the effort concurrently. A dozen magi could fill this arcane item before it reached capacity. The massive boost in potential will allow not only an individual to be translocated across the country, but an entire area filled with people, goods, or anything else we so choose!"

They were on their feet now, shouting and exuberant. Even the king was standing, clapping slowly in grand approval.

Joram stood last. He seemed terrified, but also like he was seeing her for the first time.

"If that is true, Mage Johanna, I wish to see it myself," he said, his voice cutting through the crowd from years of long practice speaking at public gatherings.

"I was hoping you would, my old mentor," she replied, a small tear working its way into her eye. Alienating the man who had been a second father to her since the time she'd been brought to the College as a child had never been part of her plan. If she could salvage that relationship in any form without compromising herself, she would.

"With the king's permission, I will require ten other volunteers."

Erich nodded, and a flurry of archmagi and magi hurried down from the stands to be part of this historic event.

Once they'd assembled near the cube, she began to address them, but was interrupted by Joram's soft but insistent voice.

"Make no mistake, this is dangerous and unprecedented work. While Mage Johanna will guide the experiment, I am the archmage in charge. If I deem the risk too high, or order it shut down for any other reason, you will comply. Immediately."

That sobered the mood, and one by one, the others all agreed with nods or words.

"That goes double for you, Johanna," he added with a profound look of disappointment on his face.

The others all looked away for a moment, suddenly awkward, as though witnessing a parent having to correct a particularly uncooperative child.

She supposed it was no more than she deserved for

going over his head publicly with the king a few minutes ago. Either way, she wasn't about to let him suck all the life from her achievement, and continued without acknowledging the rebuke.

"This will be simple for the rest of you," she began. "When I say, use a spirit spell to transfer power into the cube the same way you would for any piece of chargeable arcana. I'll be in charge of translocating us to the octant at Aramar once the cube has enough power for us all to safely make the trip. When we make the jump, expect to be disoriented for a second or two as your brain reorients to its new surroundings."

There were nods and grins all around.

"All right, let's begin."

She motioned to the cube, and one by one the others called up the Gift and began using a basic spirit spell to kick-start the process. Within seconds, they had all joined in, and Joram sighed, adding his considerable power to the cube. It began to glow green at the corners, but she expected that.

"This is incredible!" one of the others exclaimed. "The sheer reservoir of power..."

And that was the true genius of her discovery. It was unheard of. Even the oldest records, dating back before the cataclysm which had forced the desolate fleet to flee Jeranah and establish the nation of Jeranon held nothing like it. For the first time in thousands of years, the possibility existed that a spell stronger than that which a single mage, no matter how powerful, could produce, would be cast. They could finally work together, to pool their strength to accomplish... who knew what, with their combined will.

"Here we go," Johanna said, reaching out for the Gift herself and adding her own power to the flow.

She concentrated on the octant in Aramar, picturing it with its stripe of red in perfect clarity as she prepared the spell.

Click.

She drew on the cube's power and activated the spell.

The air all around them shimmered as though in a heat haze, and the sky appeared to turn a pale yellow. But that was all.

That wasn't supposed to happen. Why hadn't they moved? The translocation should only have taken an instant.

Some part of her confusion must have showed on her face, because Joram's face fell like a brick.

"End your spells," he commanded in no uncertain terms, and several of the others did so. The rest were only a second or two behind.

"End the spell, Johanna," he hissed. "Otherwise I will."

Johanna looked from the cube to Joram and back. What was happening? None of her previous trips had caused this effect.

She cursed as she stopped pouring power into the artefact. Nothing changed. The heat shimmer remained, and the sky stayed a sickly shade of yellow. She felt a thrill of fear run down her spine as the ground began shaking.

"What is happening?" the king called.

She ignored him, thinking furiously. She darted over to the stands and saw the sky was yellow there as well. This couldn't be happening. The spell shouldn't be able to exist outside the octant, and yet... She quickly returned to the others.

"Something has gone wrong," she said without preamble. This was no time for blame. She needed solutions. "The cube isn't shutting down, and the spell is encompassing a larger area than I'd intended."

"How large?" Joram asked.

"I don't know, it was supposed to be confined to the octant. The cube wasn't designed to have the ability to do anything other than act as a reservoir for the spell."

"Tell me you didn't construct an entirely new piece of arcana, girl. Tell me you just altered the limit of power from a standard design!"

Johanna's mouth opened and closed, and opened again.

Joram's eyes closed as though he were in pain, then sprung open, both furious and terrified. "The standard design, which has been in use for over a thousand years, a design which most magi never think about or alter, has fourteen safeguards built into the construct. One of them is the limit of power, which prevents a mage being sucked dry if they fall asleep whilst charging a piece of arcana. Another is the range inhibitor, which exists precisely because arcane reservoirs are by nature used to amplify the spells of their users beyond the normal expectations and limits of the caster. You might have envisioned and designed a perfect spell ending at the octant walls, but this crippled piece of garbage has no such will. It has taken your base intent and expended all the power we fed it on a single burst equivalent to that which a dozen powerful magi and archmagi could manage over the time we took to charge it up. There is no telling how far this effect will reach."

The ground trembled, and King Erich was now standing.

"What is the meaning of this?" he asked, expecting an answer.

Joram ignored him and looked at her, his face now ashen. "We have to stop this. Despite the delay, if the spell still works, we could translocate half the city. We could drop it right onto Aramar. Millions could die."

Johanna felt the blood drain from her face. This couldn't be happening! All her work, all her research, undone because she'd wanted to use arcana of her own design instead of adapting the spell which had been tried and tested for generations.

It was such a stupid, simple, prideful mistake. It made her wrong, and everything Joram had feared and cautioned her against over the years correct.

"We have to destroy it," she said.

"I assume it will explode if we damage it the wrong way?" Joram asked.

"I haven't tested that, but I assume it would be the same as any other piece of arcana and release all its energy at once if destroyed."

She thought for a long moment as strange thin lines appeared in the sky, first dozens, then thousands, all leading towards a single indefinable point.

"What is that?" one of the archmagi gasped.

"Irrelevant at this moment," Joram said as the vibration all around them spiked. The heat-like shimmer in the air was growing worse, making it difficult to see more than a few spans away.

"I think the spell is still activating," Johanna gasped. "How could it take this long? How big an area does it cover?"

Joram scowled. "Get the king out of here. Now!" He

yelled at the guards in the stands. "Evacuate the grounds!"

There was a moment of hesitation, then the stands began emptying as quickly as the occupants could be away. When an archmage of Joram's power said run, you ran.

"We're going to have to destroy it," he said to the rest of them.

"But," one of the others interjected. "It will explode."

"Yes, and probably kill us all. Maybe even the entire city. But if the spell completes itself, we'll still die, and take out the capital as well."

Johanna just stared at him, aghast. There had to be something else they could do.

"What if we fed it more power?" she said.

"More?" Joram almost choked.

"Yes, hear me out. The cube might not have all the standard fail-safes, but occasionally one will fail if powered too long or with too much power. They don't explode, they just crack and go inert. If I can trick the spell into translocating us to the same octant we are currently occupying, it might buy us time for the rest of you to break it."

Joram considered her words for a second. "It's too much of a risk. Who knows what could happen if we feed that much power into it and it doesn't go inert. We could make this much worse."

The ground trembled, throwing them all to the floor. When she stood again, she could swear the ground was on a slightly different angle.

"We're out of time. Do you have another idea?" she shouted as the others regained their feet. The lines in the sky seemed to have reoriented now, and they were definitely leading somewhere.

Joram scowled. "Maker curse you girl, you've killed us all."

Johanna felt a tear slip down her cheek as she took a shuddering breath.

"Begin," she instructed, and concentrated on keeping them in place for when the spell did activate.

The others began pouring their considerable power into the cube and it glowed again at the corners.

"Hurry!" she snapped. "The spell could trigger at any moment."

The sky turned a deep indigo as the ground shuddered again, causing a wall at the far end of the octant to crumble.

It wasn't working. The cube wasn't responding to her altered intent. It was mindless, and it had already received her instructions. Or maybe the laws of the universe didn't allow her to move to somewhere she already occupied. What else could she do? She had already killed a city. She wasn't about to kill two.

She looked around, then up at the lines in the sky. They were clearer now, all leading to a focal point... somewhere.

She concentrated on them instead. Even if it destroyed the city, it was better than landing on top of Aramar.

Click.

The translocation spell activated right as the cube cracked and failed. There was a sensation of being wrenched somewhere else, and the last thing she remembered was the sight of a tree branch rushing up towards her, and the ground far below.

"From this moment forward, no mage shall experiment with the Gift under any circumstance, except by royal decree for specific purpose. The penalty for disobedience in this matter is death."
Royal decree by King Amchin after the death of his father, King Erich Savani.

CHAPTER 22

THE CATALYST

She woke to the sight of a clear blue sky, and a flock of vultures wheeling overhead.

The pain came next. She curled up into a ball, or at least as near one as the agony in her back, arm, and side would allow.

She remembered everything. Her name, her life, the experiment. Joram's broken body, which she had laid in a line next to the others whilst having no idea who he was. His wedding ring was still in her pocket.

She sobbed. What had she done?! Had the city survived? Had it been translocated somewhere else? How far had the spell gone? Even with the extra power they'd poured into it at the end, surely the cube couldn't have amplified it across more than a neighbourhood or two at worst. She had to believe there was still hope the cube had become inert just in time to localise the effects. The split-second timing between its activation and destruction made it impossible to tell which had happened first. Maybe there was still hope that only those few of them attached to the cube by their spells had been affected. She had seen no sign of debris when she had first woken on the island. The thought gave her hope, or at least a burning need to know for sure.

She uncurled from her foetal position, every part of her body feeling as though it had been pummelled by an Imbic mutation.

"Mick!"

She sat up too quickly and her head spun. The wound in her side was still bleeding, and a large pool of red had seeped into the ground beside her.

She felt faint, but not so much that she didn't jerk back from the sight in front of her. Johanna whimpered as the sudden move tore the wound a little more. She placed a hand over it as hard as she could to stem the blood now flowing again from her side.

The Imbic which had attacked them lay not three feet from her head. It was dead, its half-cooked-chicken coloured skin now even paler than before.

She tried to get to her feet, but a wave of dizziness prevented her.

"Mick," she called more loudly. "Mick!"

There was an ominous silence in response, and she forced herself to her feet, having to lean on the Imbic's massive and disturbing corpse for support.

Her body felt utterly abused. Her arm was broken, the stab wound in her back ached fiercely, and now she had a large gash in her side where the Imbic had slammed her into a broken tree branch. And those were just the wounds which hadn't healed in the phase since the disaster.

She limped around the corner of the corpse and sat in the mud created by its fluids.

In front of her, Mick's body lay crushed beneath the

weight of the Imbic. They must have killed each other in a last violent struggle while she lay unconscious by the tree where it had felled her.

For a long time, she cried.

This was all her fault. Everyone who had died had done so because she thought she knew better than a thousand years of magi who had come before her. And she had been right. If she hadn't made that one critical mistake with the cube, the translocation spell would have worked, and none of this would have happened.

How could I have been so stupid?

"I'm sorry," she said to Mick's lifeless body, then flashed back to Aterby lying on the Kingfisher. This wasn't the first time she'd had to say those words. If she somehow survived this, she would spend the rest of her life making sure it was the last.

Whatever remained of the city was to the east. She had to make it, had to find out what had happened.

She forced herself to her feet and began shambling in that direction. Of their supplies, there was no sign. The rock Mick had placed her against had been upended during the fight, and the supplies were likely underneath. She had neither the strength nor the mental focus right now to upend the boulder with the Gift, and so she left.

How far had Mick dragged her on that makeshift stretcher? She could be dozens of leagues away, or help could be just over the next rise. The blood leaking from her latest wound wasn't slowing down, and she pressed harder, causing a whole new agony to explode in her side.

I have to keep going.

Ahead was a large patch of flattish ground dotted only by a few trees. She did her best to ascend the gentle rise, stopping every few spans to lean against a tree. She wasn't going to last long at this rate.

The lip of the rise wasn't far off. It might at least offer her a clue as to how much further she had to go.

She stumbled on, her limbs feeling heavy and sluggish as she attempted to keep moving. There was a large tree at the peak of the rise, and she kept her eyes firmly on it as she lurched onward, her mind growing fuzzy.

Johanna put one foot down, then another, and then the ground was too close.

She'd fallen to her knees. She pushed herself back to her feet more by sheer strength of will than anything else. The tree was just ahead.

She reached out and tried to make it the last few steps, but fell immediately. Her side barely hurt anymore, but she felt worse than ever. She pulled herself up as far as her hands and knees, and crawled the last two spans. When she reached the tree, she slumped into a sitting position, her back against the trunk, and looked out to the east.

She breathed in, and out, and in again. She felt nothing. To the east lay utter devastation.

It was as though the Maker had taken a great spoon and simply carved out a swath of Jeranon from horizon to horizon. The hole was larger than any lake she had ever seen, and hundreds of spans deep. She let her hand collapse to the ground. There was no help coming from the city. There was no city.

She sat there in the afternoon's last light with what remained of her thoughts. If only the island she had woken on had been to the west of the continent. Even if she had remembered everything in due time, at least she would never have had to see... this.

The city had been home to over half a million people. Who knew how many had lived in villages and homesteads on the surrounding lands?

She closed her eyes. She would be joining them soon enough. If they would have her.

The sound of horses abstractly caught her attention, and then someone was standing over her. There was a desperate expression on the soldier's face as he grabbed her by the tunic, shaking her roughly in an attempt to bring her around.

As the last of her strength fled, she swore she could see another figure standing beyond him. A tall, willowy woman dressed all in black with pale skin and hair that reached almost as low as her bare-footed ankles. The woman smiled soothingly, her full, ruby-red lips curving up as she leaned down to brush Johanna's cheek with a finger.

As death took her, the last thing she heard was the soldier shouting in terror and fury.

"What in the Maker's name happened here?! Don't you dare die, mage! What did you people do? What happened to Harverness?!"

HERE ENDS THE PATH OF PRIDE
A PREQUEL TO THE DESTROYER'S WRATH

ALSO AVAILABLE

THE DARK TEMPEST

BOOK 1 OF THE DESTROYER'S WRATH

Scan the QR code above for more information!

OUT NOW!

THE INEVITABLE SPRING

BOOK 2 OF THE DESTROYER'S WRATH

Scan the QR code above for more information!

Acknowledgments

I wrote the Path of Pride in a little under three months, and as a result not as many people were involved this time around.

First, let me say a huge thank you to my cover designer Agata Broncel from Bukovero.com, for the amazing artwork which graces the front and (on the print version) back covers of this book. In large part, the setting of the Bulwark Islands, and the way the geography and ecology affected Johanna's journey was directly inspired by this imagery.

Thank you also to Elisabeth R, who both alpha read, and then did the final proofing round in an efficient and timely fashion, allowing me to get this one out in time for a pre-Christmas release.

Finally, to anyone who has read this far, thank you for your continued support. There's no point doing this without you!

Until the next time.

Regards
N. P. Cooper

ABOUT THE AUTHOR

N. P. Cooper grew up in Melbourne, Australia, and moved to Queensland early in his twenties. He has been writing for most of his life for his own pleasure, but The Dark Tempest marks his first foray into publishing his own work. When not staring at his computer screen, he enjoys spending time with his family and friends, listening to live music, and exploring the local tidal pools with his children.

For more information on N. P. Cooper's upcoming books, appearances, and release dates, visit his website and sign up for his monthly newsletter at www.npcooper.com

FOLLOW THE QR CODE
TO WWW.NPCOOPER.COM